Also by Felix Salten

Bambi
Bambi's Children
Renni the Rescuer
A Forest World
The Hound of Florence

The CITY JUNGLE

BAMBI'S CLASSIC ANIMAL TALES

FELIX SALTEN

Translation by WHITTAKER CHAMBERS

Aladdin
New York   London   Toronto   Sydney   New Delhi

ALADDIN

An imprint of Simon & Schuster Children's Publishing Division
1230 Avenue of the Americas, New York, NY 10020
This Aladdin hardcover edition October 2014
Text copyright © 1932 by Simon & Schuster, Inc.
Jacket illustration and interior chapter spot illustrations
copyright © 2014 by Richard Cowdrey
All rights reserved, including the right of reproduction
in whole or in part in any form.
ALADDIN is a trademark of Simon & Schuster, Inc.,
and related logo is a registered trademark of Simon & Schuster, Inc.
Also available in an Aladdin paperback edition.
For information about special discounts for bulk purchases,
please contact Simon & Schuster Special Sales at 1-866-506-1949 or
business@simonandschuster.com.
The Simon & Schuster Speakers Bureau can bring authors to your live
event. For more information or to book an event contact
the Simon & Schuster Speakers Bureau at 1-866-248-3049 or visit our
website at www.simonspeakers.com.
Jacket design by Karin Paprocki
Interior design by Hilary Zarycky
The text of this book was set in Yana.
Manufactured in the United States of America 0914 FFG
2 4 6 8 10 9 7 5 3 1
Library of Congress Control Number 2014936940
ISBN 978-1-4424-8752-9 (hc)
ISBN 978-1-4424-8751-2 (pbk)
ISBN 978-1-4424-8753-6 (eBook)

The CITY
JUNGLE

Chapter One

Tikki Arrives

ON THIS PARTICULAR MORNING, in the sleeping-quarters of the orangutans' cage, Tikki was born.

It was early summer, and as the sun's first rays touched a sky aglow with pale pinks, yellows and greens, changing to a clear blue, the blackbird on the topmost branch of the tree burst into a song of joy.

All kinds of things happened in the course of that morning.

There was a domestic scene in the cage of Hella, the lioness.

Mino, the fox, had one of his attacks of insanity.

The big elephant, Pardinos, killed a boy. Nobody knew who he was or how he had managed to get into the cage.

Later, Brosso, the lion, after twelve years of service with the circus, was turned over to the zoo.

And strange and unexpected things also happened to the young wolf called Hallo.

The zoo was still: there were no human beings about. The keepers had not yet put in their appearance, and most of the animals were asleep, for, as usual, they had not slept during the night.

The trees were glorious, bathed in the sun's first rays. Their leaves were like a green and living gold. In their branches finches trilled, doves cooed, jays screeched. The oriole sped through the air, a golden flash, constantly uttering its melodious and exultant cry of love. Woodpeckers hammered, and the squirrels at their merry antics over and around the boughs, twitched their bushy red tails. There was an odor of leaves, of damp wood, of turf and of flowers blooming in their beds that were like a gay carpet. It smelled, too, of dew, of iron wet with dew, and of trim tidiness.

All the free creatures about the zoo were happy.

On the orangutans' house was an elegant weather-vane. On its very tip sat a young blackbird, singing her morning song. She had all kinds of tuneful inspirations, and grew quite drunk with her music, sitting up there as if she were alone in the world.

She knew nothing of the mother orangutan, or of little Tikki, who had just glimpsed the light of day. Indeed, she would not have understood; she would hardly have been interested. Free creatures are divided from captives by a gulf as wide as that which divides rich and poor.

Within, in the sleeping-quarters, sat Yppa, the mother orangutan, holding little Tikki in her silken black fingers.

In the two years that she had been imprisoned here with her companion she had never for a moment for-gotten her freedom.

Her home had been in the virgin jungles of Borneo. There she had grown up in the brilliant green forests, with their multitude of shapes and powerful odors. She had become daring and strong, and whether with her companions or alone, had been blissfully happy and utterly content.

Once she had gone for a stroll across a small clearing, and in the short-cropped grass discovered a quantity of bananas strewn about. Yppa squatted down and one by one industriously devoured the bananas. Heaven knows, one, or at most two, would have sufficed her. She did not suspect that human beings had strewn the bananas there, or that they contained a narcotic. She knew just one thing—she had been free and was now a captive: there had been a time when she was happy, now there was simply misery without end.

She had been overpowered by a deadening sleep. Waking, she found herself in a narrow cage surrounded by cackling, laughing humans. Her skull ached, her limbs felt numb. Terror at her plight and the loathing and the horror caused by the sight of human beings further numbed her. Her loathing increased; her horror became a kind of paralysis until both were consumed in a boundless rage.

Furiously she shook the close-set bars of her cage. She bit into the iron, butting it with her shoulder, her head.

In vain.

Exhausted, she sank down, but began all over again the next day with the same result. The days, the hours passed interminably.

By degrees Yppa's broken spirit began dimly to comprehend that the most furious rage was of no avail. She cowered in her corner, sulking. She shuddered with loathing of human beings. An uncompromising hatred of all their brood kindled in her heart. She had never done them any harm, never. She had always retreated timidly into the deepest jungle whenever she saw, or even heard or scented one.

What did the horrible creatures want of her?

They did not kill her for food. They did not beat her. They fed her fruits. But how unspeakably they tortured her by compelling her to squat day and night in that miserable barred crate. They carried her cage away from the jungle, farther and farther away, while with every day her longing for the forest devoured, gnawed, burned deeper into Yppa.

She saw streets such as she never had seen, broad plains that dismayed her, villages and cities that were a torture to her. But the most dreadful torture was the fact that everybody could watch her. All her instincts revolted. Her nature struggled desperately, with the profoundest aversion, against this abject naked exposure.

She became prudent and crafty, refusing to stir as long as it was daylight and there was a human being near. She did not pay the slightest attention to proffered delicacies but sat like a figure of bronze or wood, holding her head forlornly in her hands and concealing her face. At night she would quickly satisfy her hunger, then work passionately, with all her strength, to break open her cage. She bent one or two of the iron bars slightly, but it was hardly noticeable. Though her hands were torn, she was exhausted, and her bones, forehead and teeth ached, that was all she succeeded in doing.

But she could stretch her arm out of the cage. Secretly, when no one was looking she would clutch at freedom in this way. One day she succeeded in seizing the keeper as he offered her fresh fruit. She caught the terrified man between his neck and shoulder, pressing him against the cage until he was breathless while she spewed her desperate hate into his white face. Had she been able to force her other arm between the bars, she would have strangled the horrible creature. Had she been able to get at him with her gaping jaws, she would have torn his neck open.

She held him tightly while he screamed. Oh, what a pleasure it was to hold him so tight, to bury her nails in his skin, and see blood oozing between her fingers from the keeper's tortured flesh. She tightened her grip as the other humans rushed up shouting. Yppa was not afraid, no indeed! She gripped him more fiercely.

A sharp pain in her hand compelled her to release her victim.

It was a whip. The first time Yppa sprang up. She

was frightful as she stood erect. The long red hair on her shoulders made them seem broader. Her tousled beard, her stringy red locks, her terrible snarling jaws and fierce growls made her a terrifying monster. But behind the bars she was not dangerous. An amusing sight, no more.

The whip cracked between the bars. They were trying to beat her.

Yppa was infuriated. She snatched at the whip. Feeling the knotted leather between her fingers, she pulled once, twice, so that they had to let go at the other end. Yppa pulled the whip into the cage, and in a twinkling tore and bit and trampled it, so that the air was filled with little pieces.

A tall man interfered. "What are you doing?" he shouted.

His face was white and smooth. His clothes were white, too, and so was his sun-helmet. Yppa knew nothing about clothes or about sun-helmets. In her opinion the man looked hideous. In general, she felt the utmost aversion to these chattering creatures, who could take off their skin and put it on again, and could remove a part of their heads. Moreover, she did not understand their speech. She understood just one thing—they were enemies.

"Are you crazy?" the man shouted. "One blow was enough to make her drop him. What kind of stupid nonsense is this—punishing an orangutan! Beating her! Get out of the way, you idiots! Now she'll never become peaceable! We'll never tame her! She'll never get to trust us!"

The others drew back. The man approached the cage and spoke softly, tenderly. "Did you grab the whip? That's a good girl, Lily!"

He called Yppa "Lily."

"Did you tear up the whip? That's right, Lily. You're a fine girl, Lily, a fine girl!"

He offered her bananas, he tempted her with green figs and nuts. "Look, Lily, they're for you! Take some, Lily. See how good they taste!"

Yppa did not vouchsafe him the tiniest grimace. She sat motionless again, holding her head between her long, slender hands, hiding her face.

Meanwhile the journey continued.

These humans who were conveying Yppa had all kinds of other creatures. From time to time Yppa caught a glimpse of her companions in suffering. She could always catch their scent. There were little monkeys, parrots, a young tiger, and other inhabitants of the jungle. At night she could hear them, screeching, roaring, howling.

Yppa made no noise: she worked persistently to free herself. But gradually her hope faded.

They came to the ocean, which Yppa had never seen. She was put aboard a ship that was strange and mysterious to her. At the beginning of the voyage the cage stood on the open deck.

Yppa felt just one thing—from here she could never get back to her beloved jungle even if she succeeded in escaping from her prison. Endless water stopped her on every side. It was new to her, this water, strange, hateful. It was at this time that she finally abandoned the attempt to break open her cage.

She wept all night, quietly, perfectly quietly, and a

heart-breaking look of sorrow came into her eyes.

Later, when the air grew cooler, the sky paler, and the sun less intense, they carried the cage into the engine-room. It was hot and damp, and there was a deafening noise. Yppa suffered from the stench, from nausea, from her longing, never for a moment stilled.

For hours until she became dizzy, she would watch the rhythmical motion of the piston. She thought the bright, oil-dripping engine was a captive animal. She thought everything was captivity, inconsolable, inescapable captivity.

There followed her arrival in Europe and the torture of the train journey. When she finally reached the zoological garden Yppa was completely befuddled.

Of the garden itself she saw very little. She was brought into a warm house where she lived alone.

When the moment came for her to leave the small cage and enter the large one, she hesitated for a long while. Then she felt that the spaciousness and the mocking picture of the bare trees with the strong bare branches would be a pleasant relief. She moved about a bit, but rarely except at night. During the day she would sit with her face close to the whitewashed wall of her new prison. All day long she would rub the flakey lime from the wall with the knuckle of her middle finger.

To the people who pressed curiously about her cage, it looked as if Yppa were tracing mystic symbols and characters on the wall. Several thought that the orangutan had gone insane. And as she continued day in and day out, hesitantly but perseveringly, slowly as if under some sorrowful compulsion, to rub her knuckle (one would almost venture to say, to write) in the lime, the curator of the zoo himself inclined to the opinion that Yppa was suffering from melancholia.

She paid not the slightest attention to the human herd. She did not heed the keeper's gentle call or the tender enticements of the curator who used to come to her when she was alone, bringing her oranges, grapes and bananas, courting her as a lover his bride.

Yppa never stirred from her seat, never for one moment ceased writing with her finger. It was uncanny.

A young man who frequently visited the zoological

garden was standing beside the curator in front of the cage.

"Dreadful!" he said. "Dreadful!"

The curator smiled. "The animals are well treated in my zoo. . . ."

"No doubt," Dr. Wollet agreed. "You are a kind-hearted man, curator. And most of your colleagues are kind-hearted, amiable men. That is just what makes it so incomprehensible."

"Lily," the curator coaxed and wheedled. "Come, Lily, be a nice girl and I'll give you the nice banana."

"She'll die," said Dr. Wollet, "she'll die of a broken heart."

"What do you come here for anyway?" The curator turned on him suddenly. "What brings you here again and again?"

"Pity," said Dr. Wollet simply.

Then something unexpected happened.

Yppa rose, grasping the bare tree. A supple swing of her body and she was close to the bars. She stood erect, powerful—an elemental force. With absolute indifference and the vacuous expression of a sleep-walker she gazed past the two men, but seized the banana. Regal—a conqueror receiving an empty tribute. Indifferently she peeled the banana, and ate it neatly, but listlessly. It took scarcely three seconds. Then she again turned her back with its long red shaggy hair. One hand seized the branch. With another marvelously light swing Yppa was seated before the wall, tracing on it again with her finger.

"I'll pull her through!" the curator exulted. "I'm going to pull her through. Patience is all that is needed."

"If you stopped to think," said Dr. Wollet as he prepared to go, "if you stopped to think what prodigies of superhuman patience are performed in this zoological garden, you would never find the heart to use the word yourself."

The curator smiled at his departing back. "Sentimental bosh!" he muttered and again occupied himself with Yppa whom he insisted on calling "Lily."

One day, however, he had another narrow cage wheeled up to Yppa's prison. It was just such a cage as that in which they had brought Yppa months before. In it was a gigantic male orang.

The curator and all the keepers watched the meeting of the two creatures with bated breath.

But nothing happened.

Yppa did not move from her post by the wall. Zato, whom they called "Bobby," crouched down in one corner of his cage.

The men waited and waited. Neither animal stirred from its place.

A tremendous self-restraint, a tender and insurmountable modesty kept them from betraying to human eyes the thrilling experience of this meeting.

But the next morning they were sitting side by side. With the unconcern of affection, they sat with their arms around each other's neck and shoulders. They were silent, apparently peaceful, gazing with worried eyes into space.

This went on for days, weeks, months.

They imparted to each other the incomprehensible and terrible turn of life which had forced them into this horrible barrenness of confinement. They were stirred by the similarity of their fates, grasping only the fact that they were both unfortunate.

A gloomy wildness persisted unchanged in them, binding them one to another. They would sit motionless for hours, giving the impression that they were plunged in melancholy thought. There would follow outbreaks of hostility to their keeper—savage but not frenzied, not even angry, rather as if they were the result of mature reflection. They could not comprehend that the terrific energy with which they resisted was all in vain.

Sometimes they succeeded in escaping. In their dreams. Once more they were in the wonderful, damp, humid jungle, swinging along the lianas to the tops of the trees, shaking the fronds of the coco-palms while gigantic brilliant-colored flowers flamed around them, and huge gorgeous butterflies flashed by. A thousand bird voices screeched, cackled, tittered, whistled about them. The well-known sound of every creature that stole or galloped or fled or quarreled or rejoiced or fought, filled their ears and suffused their senses with familiar music, and they were intoxicated with a kind of happiness that only the free can feel. They enjoyed this intoxication in all its purity while they were asleep, for in their dreams they forgot their captive state.

But when sleep forsook them and they opened their eyes in the wretched restriction of their prison, they felt an unutterable despair.

It was still dangerous for their keeper, or even for the curator, to enter Yppa's and Zato's barred cell. No one had ever dared to.

But now Tikki had come.

The newborn babe rested in Yppa's raised hands, and she examined it as a merchant might consider a bit of choice ware in an oriental bazaar. For the first time in the course of her captivity something like happiness dawned palely in her soul.

Though Tikki had been on this earth a bare half hour, he seemed a thousand years old. He looked like a mummy with his meager body and scrawny neck, and especially his wrinkled face. In the sleepy, liquid expression of his eyes there was something inexplicable, unfathomable.

His mother was satisfied with him. She rocked him

in her arms and seemed about to show him to Zato. But Zato was not there. Probably they had driven him into another cage.

Yppa did not waste much time thinking about it. She applied herself to little Tikki with all the matter of fact and serious intentness of a mother orangutan. For the first time she forgot her cage, forgot her rage and rancor, forgot her bitter longing for the jungle.

Now all her powers of pacification were directed to little Tikki who stirred at his mother's breast, looking at once ineffably shrewd and pitiably helpless.

At that early hour the house in which their cage stood was empty. Neither the curator nor any of the keepers had yet put in his appearance.

But Yppa was not alone with Tikki.

She had a tiny observer, one so tiny, indeed, that Yppa did not even notice her. Two eyes, hardly bigger than a pin-head, dark, sharp and clever, eagerly followed every movement of the mother and child.

In a little crack where the floor of the cage joined the wall sat Vasta the mouse.

She had often sat in that crack, certain that she was not observed, yet trembling each time with excitement. After the spectacle that she had just witnessed, she trembled more excitedly than ever.

Of course, nature had designed her to be timid, to tremble and to flee. But here in the zoological garden where so many big animals lived in captivity, Vasta knew the pride of a free creature and was on a fairly familiar footing with all the imprisoned beasts. Though she never forgot that caution with which a mouse is born, she did in time get over her dreadful fear of all the huge forms among which she crept.

She learned that the imprisoned animals were either too good-tempered or too unhappy to harm a tiny mouse.

But these orangutans remained mysterious and uncanny. She was perpetually horrified by their resemblance to the most dangerous and most powerful creature the mouse knew.

Nevertheless, she often visited the orangs. She was drawn by curiosity and probably, too, by the partially eaten nuts that were always lying about. But principally she was lured on by the terror she felt whenever she gazed at the orangutans.

Never could she make up her mind to reveal herself. And she always slipped away with the blissful shuddery feeling of having escaped some horrible fate.

That day she remained longer than usual. She was so spellbound by the event she had witnessed that she never once thought how safely she could have hunted for nuts.

Her sharp nose twitched violently, her majestic whiskers quivered, her whole body was trembling when at last she ran away.

Chapter Two

"Come On Out, Boys!"

SOFT, AND FILLED WITH THE CHARM
and grace of developing life in young bodies,
Barri and Burri were playing together. They
rejoiced in the age of four weeks which had
been one uninterrupted round of pleasure, one huge
entertainment.

Their mother, the lioness Hella, sat with her forepaws stretched out before her, her handsome head with

its keen but tender expression raised to watch the antics of her children.

Quite suddenly, Barri lay down, as if tired—and he really may have been somewhat exhausted. He needed so little preparation to lie down, was so mobile, so elastic and loose in all his joints, that he seemed suddenly to have given way in a heap as he sprawled on the floor. He had a roguish expression and suppressed a smile.

Burri stumbled over his brother's unexpected form, tumbling down as if he had no bones at all. He picked himself up somewhat confused, taking his brother's calm repose as a new challenge. In any case, he had no intention of allowing a pause in the sport. He trotted up to Barri and cuffed his ear.

Barri parried from where he lay, a quick stroke that caught his assailant on the leg. Burri jumped on him. It was a hop-skip-jump which met a response of childish playfulness that was like a silent exultation. But Burri came instantly prancing back again and tapped his playmate's flank with a paw which was much too big for him and which it would quite evidently take him some time to grow up to.

Barri rolled over on his back, waving all four feet in the air. The little fellow was laughing fit to burst, laughing not merely with his face but with his whole body.

Burri stood over him. The two began to tussle. Lying on his back, Barri resisted, pressing his hind-legs against Burri, and finally succeeded in taking a fall out of him though for a moment his brother had looked like the victor. Then they rolled into a ball together, kicking and snapping. This was followed by gentle growls and snarls.

It was all fun and, as children, it delighted them to play in this fashion. But in the depths of their natures, not quite awakened as yet, an untamable wildness vibrated and was tested in these playful struggles.

Mother Hella watched them with majestic satisfaction. She laughed.

There was another spectator, too—Vasta the mouse. She sat by the partition that separated their pen from the outer cage. When she saw the lioness laugh, she plucked up courage.

"Splendid children!" she piped.

Hella pricked up her ears and turned her head. "You here again?"

"I just ran in for a moment," said Vasta.

"Any news?" asked the lioness.

"My dear!" She sat up on her hind-legs, holding her neat forepaws under her little pointed nose. "Something quite remarkable."

She was about to begin her story when Burri and Barri, who heard her, came trotting over, their heads cocked, bent on mischief, side by side. They crouched, began to slink, prepared to spring. Here was a new plaything.

But Vasta was disinclined to be a plaything for young lions. She flashed through the crack by which she had come. Burri and Barri pawed clumsily at the spot where the mouse had been. Eagerly they sniffed at the crack of Vasta's refuge. Heads down, they scratched impatiently at the bottom of the wall, whimpering, "Come out! Come on out!"

Vasta, however, declined the invitation. But she was

unable to withstand the urgency of their pleadings, and presently piped politely, "I'm not here!"

Barri and Burri rushed to their mother. "She won't come out," Barri whispered in her ear.

Burri, who had squatted down on his hams, addressed himself to his mother with a very serious mien. "She says she's not there!"

Thereupon Barri began to tug at his mother's ear and neck while Burri at once applied himself to Hella's full and beautiful jowl.

The lioness uttered deep, gurgling sounds of inward satisfaction and great tenderness. She interspersed them with growls of apparent crossness.

The cubs did not believe her for a moment. In fact they were delighted. This flirting with the fringes of maternal fury was the best fun in the world. They pressed upon their mother more furiously, sprang at her throat, shoved their big soft paws against her nose, her face, fastened their teeth in her neck, and were perfectly wild with joy because they imagined that they were stronger than she. Of course, she knew that this strength of theirs was pure fancy, but that did not diminish her joy.

With a roar of delight the lioness rolled over on one side. The tassel of her tail beat the floor softly. There was a wonderful supple grace in her powerful body as, yielding to the cubs' impudence, she rolled now on her back, now on her flank.

Visitors to the zoological garden had crowded to the cage to watch this family scene. They chattered, and shouted various expressions of approval to the lioness. One youth beat his cane against the bars of the cage. It made a shrill metallic sound. Hella did not pay the slightest attention. She was accustomed to being stared at and was contemptuously indifferent. Only immediately after Burri's and Barri's appearance in the world had she been somewhat sensitive. But the curator, who knew the nervousness of animals that have just become mothers, had the front of her cage boarded up. Hella was alone with her children for a whole week, free from all disturbance.

Now she was perfectly unembarrassed in her delight in her cubs. Sometimes she flung them off, or pressed them to the floor, or drew them lovingly into her embrace or let herself be overpowered by Burri and Barri in sport.

But now, while he was still at a distance, she heard the keeper's footstep.

She was expecting him, and at the first sign of his approach, interrupted the fun to sit erect, quieting the children, who tottered about confused until they perceived that their mother was aroused and waiting. Imitating her, they sat upright with old shrewd faces, but quite perplexed.

The lioness bared her teeth, drawing back her jowls and uttering a thin, piping sound. Suddenly she snapped her beautiful mouth shut and repeated the sound. Her tail kept twitching and waving. It was a sign of impatience, irritation. She rose and paced up and down the cage. At the bars she turned, tossing her head up, then down, in an eloquent gesture of powerlessness. She turned in an incredibly small space, slinking with all her restrained and terrible strength visible in her limbs, close to the bars, from one side of the cage to the other. Back again and back again and back again. Ten times, twenty times.

Finally she stopped in one corner as if rooted there, staring out intently, always in one direction, lashing her flanks softly with her constantly waving tail. Her eyes were phosphorescent. Then her rigidly shut expression distorted itself into a furious snarl, which grew louder and louder.

The keeper was standing in front of the cage.

"There, there," he called to Hella, "don't get worked up. I'll bring them back to you. You know I will. I'm not stealing them. Don't get upset, old girl."

It did not calm Hella in the least. She struck at the man with her terrible paw so that all the bars reverberated.

Meanwhile the keeper, with the help of his prod, had raised the small door to the empty adjoining cage and was enticing the cubs.

Barri slunk over.

The lioness bounded into the air, clutching at him with her paws, and growling, "Stay here!"

But the confused and faithless cub did not listen.

Burri was wavering. The keeper thrust the long ironshod pole into Hella's cage, trying to poke him out. "Come on, boy," he kept urging, "come along! We'll go out in the fields and get some sun!"

Hella attacked the pole in a white rage. The keeper laughed. "You don't mean that, mother. You don't begrudge the little fellows their fun. You'll get them back again."

Hella bit at the iron that was prodding Burri, threw the whole weight of her body against it and forced it to the floor.

The keeper was patient. "Come on," he said to her, "always the same old antic."

Burri meanwhile had crept beside his brother. The keeper withdrew the pole, closing the little low door with it. Opening the empty cage in which the cubs were now squatting, he climbed in and gathered them up in his arms.

The lioness stood with lowered head, panting. A shudder passed over her spine and flanks. When she saw her cubs in human hands a pitiable howl broke from her chest.

The keeper turned to her. "Be easy, be easy, I'll bring them back to you. My word of honor."

A peal of laughter rose from the crowd of spectators.

The lioness lay down again and was silent. But her mouth hung open, her tongue lolled, and it was plain to see from her heaving flanks how upset and anxious she was. But she betrayed it by no other sign. She lay motionless and quiet as the keeper climbed out into freedom with Burri and Barri. Nor did she stir as he set the cubs on the floor and walked off with them. All the spectators followed.

Vasta emerged from her crack.

"I'm surprised," she said meekly, "really surprised at the way you take on every time."

There began one of those conversations which are constantly occurring between creature and creature. Humans heed only the sounds that animals make. Hence their observations remain superficial. Man pays no attention at all to those expressions, gestures, motions that go to make up the language of the beasts, so that he almost never understands them, although one would think that, after thousands of years, he might have learned something about them, even with his atrophied instincts. That is why the tiny brothers by whom we are surrounded remain speechless as far as man is concerned, and why we think it a considerable advance if he even begins to regard them as brothers. In no other way is it possible to explain, if not to understand, how human beings can perpetrate such tortures, such incredible, inhuman tortures, upon living creatures—spiritual as well as physical sufferings and tragedies that deprive life of its joy and torment the dreams of all who are conscious of them.

Hella the lioness rested her beautiful head on her outstretched forepaws. Her big, golden eyes gazed, full of gentle trouble, into space. "I don't know what He is up to," she said.

"Don't worry," Vasta was eager to comfort her. "He takes them out in the fields. There are lots of His kind there, and they all look and laugh and are very nice to the little ones."

"I don't know what He is up to," Hella repeated.

"He'll bring them back again. He always brings them back."

The lioness smiled. "They'll smell of fresh grass."

"Then why are you so worried?"

The sparkle died in Hella's eye. "I had children once before."

"You don't say! I didn't know anything about that," Vasta sputtered.

"You weren't here then. Since then the trees have twice been green and bare again. I was so young in those days."

"Ah!" Vasta drew a little nearer. "I wasn't even in the world in those days."

"Little mouse," said Hella, turning her head, "you see much more than I do, much more, but you know much less."

Vasta polished her nose briskly and said nothing.

"I had three charming children," Hella continued,

"remarkably handsome children. I loved them desperately. Yes, I love them even today; I can't forget them."

"Where are they?" interrupted Vasta.

"I don't know," growled the lioness. "He took them to the meadow every day, just as He does Burri and Barri. One day He returned alone without the children! It was terrible!"

Both were silent for a while. Hella was crying.

"What can He have done with them?" Vasta pondered.

"No one knows," whispered Hella. "Three splendid children—gone! Three at one swoop! One never knows, never will know, what He is up to. Now I am afraid again, afraid for Burri and Barri." She got up and began to pace back and forth behind the bars.

Vasta wanted to change the subject. "Yppa has a son," she said.

The lioness halted. "At last she'll be happy."

"It really looks that way. She's sitting there very quiet, hugging the little thing. She's quite taken with it."

"That's good," said Hella. "That was what she needed.

That will console the poor thing for her lost freedom." Hella rose, her whole body trembling softly. "Freedom..." She grew thoughtful. "I never knew what it is to be free. In spite of all that you and others tell me, I really believe that there isn't any other world but this garden. I know nothing but this space shut off by those black bars and that other smaller room, inside, where I stay when it's cold. And I'm content. Sometimes I feel very good, some-times I'm even happy and cheerful when I'm lying in the warm sun, and especially when I'm with Pono or some other member of the family. Or when I'm with the children."

She stopped and stretched herself.

"But there are other times," she began again reso-lutely, "when I feel a terrible pang of longing, I don't know what for!" She drew nearer to Vasta and whis-pered, "You belong outside there, little one, tell me the truth—what is freedom?"

Vasta was embarrassed, she cowered and stam-mered: "I can't answer that. Freedom is freedom, that's all, and it may not be such a great piece of good fortune as Yppa and some of the rest of you think. One is constantly in danger. One has to be forever on guard."

"You are clever, little one." Hella nodded. "Very clever. I don't want your freedom."

"I'm going," said Vasta.

"Come again soon," purred the lioness, "come and bring me the latest news. I'm always glad to listen to you."

"If I live," promised Vasta, and whisked away.

A little later the lioness sprang to the bars, standing as motionless as a statue as she swung her tail in circles for joy. Burri and Barri were returning, surrounded by a dense crowd of people.

But Hella saw only her cubs. She was blissfully happy.

Chapter Three

An Elephant, a Goat and a Dead Boy

THE POOR LAD IS DREADFULLY torn up!"

In the elephant house, which had been closed to the public, the curator, his two assistants and several keepers were gathered about a dead boy. Even Eliza, who took care of the chimpanzees, had stolen in.

The body, which was hanging between the bars crushed to a pulp, was that of a person who had not quite outgrown his boyhood. It was well-dressed, though they could scarcely tell that, for the clothes were fluttering in tatters from the limbs.

All of them were laboring to disengage the lifeless form from the bars between which it was wedged as if in powerful pincers. They succeeded after much vexation and rough handling that made all of them shudder. Now it was lying on the stone pavement, as the curator, bending over it, muttered in a tone of mingled pity, horror and anger, "The poor lad is dreadfully torn up!"

Meanwhile the elephant stood innocently by, as if nothing had happened, or as if, in any case, he were perfectly guiltless. As usual when he was in a good humor he rocked his huge gray body from side to side with a uniform motion. With a nonchalance that seemed shameless to the group of men, he would take little handfuls of hay from his manger, draw them through his soft rubbery mouth, then drop them on the floor.

The curator started up and approached the cage. He was perfectly pale, shocked and angry at the same time.

"I suppose, curator," said one of the assistants,

indicating Pardinos, "that we'll have to shoot that fellow."

The curator waved aside the remark.

"Yes," the other assistant rallied to the support of his colleague. "Remember that he's already seriously injured one keeper–Joseph."

"Silence!" cried the curator in a rage. "Silence! Joseph indeed! It was his own fault! He tormented the elephant! Unfortunately I found it out too late or I'd have discharged him in time! Shoot the elephant! Because he was violent ten years ago and has behaved himself nobly ever since!"

He glanced around, then pointed to an old keeper. "Well, Philip," he commanded sharply, "why so tongue-tied? Go ahead and talk! You know what happened! Tell it!"

"Well," the old man began awkwardly, "he could have trampled Joseph that time."

"Go on," growled the curator.

"But he simply picked him up and dashed him down."

"Go on!" The curator stamped his foot. "What did he do to Joseph?"

"He broke a couple of his ribs," the old man explained. "But that's all. As for him," Philip pointed to the elephant, "the tip of his trunk was all raw. Something had been done to him."

"And in all the ten years that came after he's done nothing worse than in the ten years that went before." The curator was tremendously excited. "William!" He turned to an old keeper. "How long have you taken care of the elephants?"

"Seven years," said William.

"And?" The curator was bursting with rage.

"And," William continued, "Hans has been the best-tempered of them all."

These humans called Pardinos "Hans."

William was about to smile, but recollected that he was in the presence of a corpse, and pointed to the cage. "Think how he loves Minka."

They all glanced in, as astonished as if they had never known this before, unable to reconcile the gentleness of the elephant with what had happened.

A little white goat had bounced out of one corner of

the cage and was rubbing against the huge columns of the colossus' legs, munching the straw that he scattered.

This was Minka.

The curator walked to the bars with a determined air. "Open the cage!" he ordered William.

They all crowded about the curator in terror.

"For God's sake!"

"You're risking your life!"

"Don't go in there with him now, he's aroused."

Eliza screamed. "Oh, God, I can't bear to see it!" But she did not stir from the spot.

"Bosh!" said the curator. "Quiet!" And when they had all fallen silent, he commanded again emphatically, "Open the cage, William, at once!"

The keeper unbarred the cage: the curator entered. He walked straight up to the elephant, who at first pretended not to notice anything. When the curator was right beside him, Pardinos turned very slightly, a decorous turn, so that man and beast were face to face with one another.

"Look here, you blackguard," the curator began in a

level voice which nevertheless vibrated with grief and excitement. "You loathsome blackguard, you've committed a murder, a common cruel murder. Yes, look at your miserable victim!" He pointed outside where the corpse lay surrounded by the men. "Why did you do it?"

This was a real question, demanding and seeming to await a real answer.

The curator was all but weeping. "I took you for a good honest fellow. I was your friend. You! I would never have believed it of you."

The elephant blinked and there was a trace of embarrassment discernible in the shifty glance of his long-lashed human eyes. He swung his trunk to the right and left like the pendulum of a huge clock. But in the lifted corners of his lower lip there was something like a covert smile.

The curator half turned to the men outside, supporting himself with one hand against the elephant's forehead. "Remove the body quietly! And inform the authorities."

They covered the dead boy with sail-cloth, and

making an unrecognizable parcel of him, heaved him on a hand-car and trundled him off.

"Philip and William, you stay here," commanded the curator. "You, too," he shouted after one of the keepers. Then he turned to the elephant again.

"Do you know that you'll probably have to be shot? Have you gone mad, old fellow? The penalty for murder is death! Even for a great lord like you. Which is just as it should be!"

"But he's perfectly peaceable!" It was Eliza's anxious voice.

"Silence!" commanded the curator.

She was still, frightened at her own outcry.

"Are you going to maul me?" the curator continued. "Or kill me? Me? After we've hit it off so well for nearly twenty-five years!"

The elephant did not stir, but continued to sway his trunk back and forth.

"Well, we'll see," said the curator, slapping the elephant's gray iron-like forehead as he spoke. "We'll see, my friend, how things stand with you! We'll see whether you're in your right mind or ripe for a bullet."

"Be careful now!" he commanded the tensely listening men in a low voice. "The hooks! But don't let him see you!"

Cautiously William and Philip fetched two steel prods, a long and a short one, whose points were as sharp as needles. They came nearer.

"Stay outside," the curator ordered. "Watch every motion! And if you have to, let him have it in the eyes and trunk."

Suddenly he stooped and snatched at Minka.

She eluded him with a short bleat. As the curator started to chase her the elephant became wildly excited. His huge ears clapped up and down with a rustling noise. He raised his trunk high, and a piteous sound issued from his gaping red mouth, like the tone which issues from a trumpet blown by an inexperienced trumpeter.

The curator did not relax his pursuit of Minka. Pardinos placed himself squarely across his path. His trunk swished wildly through the air as if it were seeking some support, his ears clapped up and down incessantly. The broken poignant tones kept issuing from his throat.

Presently Philip and William were compelled to enter the cage.

The curator walked around the elephant and tried to catch Minka.

With a sudden lightning-quick movement, Pardinos threw himself on the floor between Minka and the curator. It was a powerful gesture of unconditional obedience and passionate entreaty.

The curator swung himself over the mountain of Pardinos' body, caught the goat, took her in both arms, and carried her, walking close to the wall, past Pardinos, to the entrance.

Once more the elephant was on his feet. But he made no move to follow the curator. He stood rooted to the spot, stricken as if by a blow of fate.

Accompanied by Philip and William, the curator left the cage.

"That settles it," he burst out as he set down Minka. She immediately bounded over to the cage.

"Catch her," muttered the curator. Eliza crouched down and clasped the goat gently, whispering words of consolation to her.

The curator mopped his forehead, cheeks and neck with his handkerchief. It was not until then that his heart began to throb so that he could hear it pounding in his throat and temples. It was then, when it was all over, that he realized how upset he had been.

"Well?" he asked, with a glance of inquiry at the others. "Well? Does either of you dare say now that the old fellow is dangerous? Or that he ought to be shot?"

Neither answered.

The elephant came up to the bars, stretching his trunk longingly after Minka whom he could not reach, but who bleated to him. Both animals were dismayed by the separation, were unhappy and filled with fear. But the elephant seemed to be thinking no more of violence than Minka herself.

"When you have to shoot," said the curator, "then shoot! But only when you have to. It's frightful enough then! Almost as frightful as hanging a murderer." He added softly after a pause, "It has always been especially shocking to me, because such a person is judged only by our human standards, but by those of nature he is always innocent. Always innocent!"

His voice trembled as he pronounced the last words.

The elephant, his huge head pressed against the bars and his trunk extended, uttered a sobbing cry. His gestures, his expression, his eyes—all held an uncanny, urgent, eloquent appeal.

"Yes, old fellow," said the curator, "you're crying, aren't you? If I really wanted to punish you, I'd take Minka away for all time."

The elephant's cry roared mightily through the empty tiled room.

As if in response, the curator himself cried out: "I know! She's the only friend you have in the world! But you don't realize that you've destroyed the only joy of some poor parents. That you don't know."

The elephant's expression was that of a desperate prisoner. He really seemed to feel remorse. Actually he felt nothing of the kind. He simply wanted his little darling, Minka the goat. He desired her presence with all that terrible energy of his whole being which animals put into their wants.

The curator rubbed his hands together nervously, cracking his knuckles. "We mustn't excite him too much," he decided, "or make him needlessly wild. We may have to repeat this test before the authorities. Let the goat go!"

Eliza stood up and the goat ran to the cage. She was so small that she easily slipped between the bars to Pardinos.

He saw that she was coming and received her with a transport of discreet tenderness. The goat ran round the elephant's legs, one after the other, rubbing herself against the four iron-gray columns. Meanwhile the elephant was dancing slowly, apparently quite deliberately, raising his broad thick foot a little distance from the floor and setting it down again with surprising gentleness. He had swung his trunk high as if he meant to break the goat into pieces, but he brought it down very softly, running the finger at the tip in a breathy caress over Minka's head and back. He exulted in the process, so that it sounded as if a gush of water were gurgling through a suddenly open pipe.

Side by side, the goat looked even smaller and the elephant more gigantic. It was grotesque.

"I wonder how that poor fellow managed to get in, and if he was hidden here all night," said the curator. "We'll have to have a thorough investigation; it must absolutely be explained." With that he left.

But in spite of his thorough investigation, nothing was explained.

Chapter Four

In Peter's House

ELIZA HAD SUDDENLY DISAPPEARED after releasing Minka. She hurried to Peter the chimpanzee, with whose care she was entrusted and whom she loved like a child.

She was crying quietly as she looked after the wants of the clever, cheerful monkey.

Eliza knew something about the tragic event. Not all, but enough to make her shed a few self-reproachful tears. Nor did she restrain them because there were visitors already standing before the glass front of the cage. Let them think what they liked. Even if one was only the girl who sat all day long with the chimpanzees, one could feel vexed or sorry. Whose business was it anyhow?

Eliza was the only person in the zoo who knew the name of the unfortunate boy. She took good care not to divulge her knowledge. A vague shyness kept her from it.

His name had been Rainer Ribber, and he had never been numbered among fate's fortunates. "Mr. R.-R.," she called him when they talked together. "Dear R.-R.," of late, and as a joke. They were done with joking now.

Peter the chimpanzee sat before Eliza, observing her with his big professorial eyes. He pursed the black lips of his strong protruding mouth. Whenever he did that, he looked as if he were about to make some sagely humorous remark. But he never said anything and had to keep all his epigrams to himself. He understood that Eliza was sad. To cheer her up, he selected a doll from among his playthings, a black Pierrot, seized it by the arm and threw it gently at Eliza.

A challenge to play.

Eliza remained unmoved. The doll slipped from her lap, fell to the floor and lay with its arms outspread like the dead lad in the elephant house.

Eliza looked down at the Pierrot. "Ah, Peter," she said, "you will never see poor, good R.-R. any more. Never again will he bring you bananas and grapes. He is dead."

Peter scratched his head reflectively and turned a quiet somersault.

Eliza gazed at him, her eyes filmed with tears.

For almost a year she had been taking care of this good-natured funny fellow. When she came he had been nervous and quarrelsome; now he was quiet and tractable. He had lain sick in her arms. But for several months now he had been well and happy. The little monkey, always up to some knavish prank or other, possessed as tender and gentle a soul as the very best children to whom Eliza had been nurse. He had never angered her, never done anything to spite her, never put on airs before her, like so many human children. Behind his low brow, or (who can really say?) perhaps in his hairy black breast, there was hidden a pious gratitude for Eliza, a boundless trust in his keeper, a feeling so powerful that no other could compete with it.

Peter got up and came over to Eliza, walking erect on his flat feet. He looked as if he were trying to think of some means of cheering her up. Suddenly he sprang on the big wooden ball that lay in his path, and, started it rolling, balancing delicately, danced on it.

The crowd of people who were waving and applauding outside the cage he ignored entirely. His eyes peered quickly at Eliza, who continued to weep quietly.

Instantly Peter grasped one of the flying rings, and swinging himself over, clambered up to the roof. For a while he crouched there, dangling, then with a terrific plunge he was on the floor again in front of Eliza.

Outside from the visitors came a many-voiced cry of fear. Peter merely blinked contemptuously. He crouched down, and laying his long arms carefully in Eliza's lap, gazed pityingly at her.

Eliza stroked his head wearily and sighed. "Ah, my good Peter, what can you know after all?"

She remembered how, about two years ago, the curator had been the guest of Dr. Wollet where she was employed as a nurse. "If you ever leave your situation," he said to her, "come to me, I may have a place for you." Later she had left the Wollet children, and recalling the curator's invitation, came to see him, quite unaware that he wanted her for Peter, the chimpanzee. But she had said yes, and until today had had no regrets.

Peter sat up, and flinging his arms around her neck, drew her down to him and with lips absurdly pursed kissed her cheek. A kiss as soft as a sigh, a pathetically understanding kiss.

Raucous laughter. Eliza resisted gently with, "That's enough, thanks, Peter." She recalled how long it had been before Peter had bestowed the same mark of favor on nice Rainer Ribber.

Poor R.-R.! She wept more bitterly. He was so modest, so terribly shy, that he infected others with his own embarrassment. And yet he had such determination, knew so definitely what he loved and what he hated. Oh, yes, he could hate, too. Eliza had often been afraid when he said grimly, "I don't like him!" as he shut his eyes and his features grew tense. Once he had said it so fiercely behind Karl's back that Eliza had started in fright. For Karl's sake she was hurt by the words. For there were all kinds of delicate threads binding Karl and her, and some day, perhaps, they would be married.

Karl was the keeper of the bears. He was a strong and stocky fellow, not very tall, with a robust, healthy outlook. He often used to visit Eliza in the chimpanzee house, and sit there or help in all sorts of ways, and they had become close friends.

Then the delicate boyish youth had come. He had appeared for the first time two months before. He would stand outside the glass all day long with the other visitors, but usually at times when the zoological garden was empty. Eliza had not wanted to let him into the cage. But he had been so insistent, so shy but so polite. "Ah, please, miss," he had said, "only for a minute. Let me stay with the good creatures for just a minute. It will do me so much good; it will be such a comfort to me." He had stuttered and stammered over the last words. Eliza could not refuse him further.

"Comfort?" she had asked him. "What do you need comfort for?"

He answered evasively, and turned to Peter. His way of approaching the young chimpanzee, of winning his affection, and playing with him, revealed so much good feeling, such deep understanding, that not only Peter, but Eliza also, began to trust him entirely.

When after a few minutes Rainer had wanted to go, Eliza said, "You may stay." And he stayed.

Indeed, he kept coming back and brought playthings and lovely fruit, carried Peter in his arms and hugged him. He would give up without resistance anything that the chimpanzee, ransacking his pockets, wanted.

Peter ruined Rainer's watch, he tore his handkerchief, his memorandum book, he wound his necktie around his neck, pulled out his cufflinks, and threw his money on the floor. Rainer never even smiled, was never impatient.

Eliza sympathized with him, but gradually felt a kind of jealousy.

"You let him make a fool out of you," she said irritably.

Rainer looked surprised, but merely shook his head.

Eliza was insistent. "You let the creature tyrannize over you too much."

"Too much?" he asked, still more surprised. "Since the world began, the only tyranny has been that of men over the beasts." He gazed gloomily into space. "Cruel . . . pitiless . . ." A sigh. Then silence.

Eliza was silent, too. She was disarmed.

Later he told her in confidence why he had needed comforting.

"My squirrel died. Oh, no, I didn't catch it, I bought it from an animal dealer, because I couldn't bear to watch it rushing around in his cage. I wanted to free him. But he was unsuited for a life of freedom. Absolutely helpless! So I took him back home with me. I kept him in my room—at least it wasn't a cage. We became great friends."

He would not say more and never mentioned it again.

When Eliza sought to elicit certain details a few days later, he said shortly, "You know all there is to know."

Usually he visited the chimpanzees in the morning or in bad weather. In any case he always appeared when there were very few or no people at all in the zoo.

Once he met Karl just as the latter was finishing his chat with Eliza. "I don't like him," he had said the moment Karl was gone. It had shocked Eliza, but she did not dare object.

Now she recollected that a few weeks before, Rainer had let fall a chance remark: "One must be alone with the animals. It's best at night when they are awake. They never sleep at night . . . the unfortunate creatures. That's the time to be with them."

She had paid no particular attention then, but now

the words struck her, as did also the passionate manner in which Rainer had uttered them.

She was recalling the previous evening. Rainer had been late in visiting Eliza and Peter, late and quite unexpected. It was already deep twilight and all the people had left the zoo. Peter was lying wrapped up in his covers, sleeping. Rainer tiptoed to the little chimpanzee's bed, bent over it and gazed at him steadily.

"I had to see you like this, too, my good friend," he had murmured, "like this, too." With that he had gone.

Eliza went out and stood in front of the monkey house; she thought she could make out Rainer dodging among the shrubbery. But she could not see him very clearly. For a moment she was taken aback. Was Rainer dodging into the shrubbery in order to conceal himself? Then she smiled at the idea. All the keepers had bloodhounds and made the rounds of the zoological garden during the night. Rainer Ribber knew that as well as Eliza.

Peter climbed out of his cage, and rummaging about the room behind it, lugged back some garments—

his uniform, a coat of ruddy cloth with gold epaulettes, and blue trousers with gold trimmings. He wanted her to dress him up. Much as Peter pretended to despise his public, he was bent on making an impression. With all his tricks and playful pranks he managed to maintain the appearance of proud indifference. But it was easy to see what pains he took to produce an effect, and how much the applause, the laughter and shouts of the crowd increased his good humor and fed his ambition to succeed in comedy.

Eliza took the clothes indifferently as Peter stood expectantly before her. She heard herself saying to Rainer Ribber, "You let him make a fool of you." She could have smiled.

Rainer had become worse than a monkey's fool. He had become the fool of death.

Suddenly Eliza saw it all clearly. Rainer really had concealed himself. Too late she saw him slipping into the shrubbery. Too late she realized that he knew the keepers' rounds and how to avoid them. Too late she was convinced that those were Rainer's footsteps she had heard that night, some time between three and four. She had awakened for a few moments and heard steps outside. Ah, now she realized that they had been far too light, far too cautious for a keeper's, as she had thought in her drowsiness. They had departed far too lightly, too discreetly.

Peter pawed at her, a gentle demand.

Eliza assisted the chimpanzee into his uniform. He buttoned the coat himself, and playfully undid all those that Eliza had buttoned. He kept this up for some time.

"I could have saved him," thought Eliza, busying herself with the monkey.

"I could have saved him twice, in the early evening and that time at night."

She recalled Rainer's fantastic love for the black panther who was so fiercely savage that nothing could break or tame him. He would tear at the bars of his cage until exhaustion forced him to lie down.

Had it been the black panther that tore Rainer to pieces that night, Eliza would have felt differently about it. Of course, there would have been the same regret, the same pangs of conscience that pained her now. But it would have been easier to submit to the dark destiny that had swept away the mysterious lad.

But the elephant? The best-natured beast in the zoo? Eliza shuddered.

She dismissed Peter, whose toilette was completed, and leaving the cage, went to the anteroom. There she could not be observed from the outside.

With a magnificent gesture, the equal of his gorgeous costume, Peter swung himself into his little wooden automobile, and seizing the wheel and treading hard on the pedals, rushed madly around in a circle. There was humor in his driving.

Eliza sat down on the bench where she had so often sat with Rainer Ribber or Karl. She dried her eyes, for she could weep no more. She felt a dreadful anxiety. A sense of guilt, of cruel punishment tormented her heart.

She was implicated in this tragedy, for it had been

in her power to prevent it twice. She could not under-stand it all. She sat staring fearsomely into space.

Her one thought was: Don't say anything. Don't tell anybody.

The door rattled. Karl came in. "Don't say a word even to him!" thought Eliza as she returned his greeting.

"Well," said Karl, "what about tonight?"

Eliza did not answer.

"Tonight," said Karl, "you and I are going out!" There was a firm satisfied tone in his voice. "We can go to Luna Park." He stretched himself comfortably. "We'll be with people for a change, not always among beasts!" He paused for a moment, then added, "I look forward to the dancing."

"I'm not going out," said Eliza dully.

He started. "Why?"

"I'm not going dancing tonight!"

"What's the matter?" he asked fiercely. "What's the matter with tonight?"

"You know what's the matter," she said.

"That's got nothing to do with you." Karl was angry.

Eliza trembled. She bowed her head. "I feel miserable."

Karl was pressing. "All the more reason for trying to enjoy yourself."

But Eliza was firm. "I mustn't enjoy myself. I can't. I feel miserable."

Chapter Five

The Curator

FOR A LONG TIME THE CURATOR HAD cherished the plan of taking his vacation in the spring and wandering alone through the countryside and forest as he used to do. A student, connoisseur and reverent lover of nature, he was as accustomed to the wild solitudes of the north as of the tropics. Indeed he never really felt solitary. That stirring life which had surrounded him from his youth in the forests of his native country, the turbulent life in

Central Africa, in the Indian jungles or in the wilds of other lands, that wonderful, mysterious, eventful life to which all his senses were perfectly attuned, prevented him from ever feeling lonely. Now that he was responsible for this zoological garden and its inhabitants, he felt at times a desire to wander in the nearby woods, to seek there something which, even though it was supervised, yet seemed to approach a primitive state. He loved to tramp over hill and dale and through the thickets, to stand in the wind, to watch, to listen, as he had in his roving years.

He was about to get into the automobile standing before the zoo gates. "Ah," he thought, "freedom at last!"

But the word "freedom" recalled to his mind Dr. Wollet who always had such violent things to say against the imprisonment of wild animals. So much that was false, sentimental, wrong-headed, as the curator thought.

He hesitated, then muttering a distracted "Wait" to the chauffeur, turned back to the zoo. Hesitating, he passed through the wide gates, hastening his pace a little so that the keepers who greeted and stared at him would think that he was called back by some official duty. Then he began to saunter more slowly along the short, but very broad, elm-bordered walk. The elms were healthy. Their wide-spreading branches possessed that strength the mere sight of which lends repose and confidence.

Shrill screeches, harsh half-articulated shrieks, shattered in their effort to form speech, drew the curator's attention from the tree tops. Parrots. Beating their wings, the brilliant birds sat chained to perches, almost as tall as a man, among the trees. They climbed deliberately and slowly up their perches and down again. Stately macaws, dark blue, deep red, orange yellow, with powerful hooked beaks. White cockatoos, the crests of many of them touched with a very light yellow, like pure unalloyed gold. When they raised these crests, they looked like grotesque clowns, droll but impudent. All these birds had remarkable faces, and the play of their features was astonishingly mobile. They were full of character, these faces, stern, arch, irate, good-natured,

alive with dangerous malice, amusing cunning, a childish delight in play, grudging and repellant pride. There
was something, too, profoundly sage in all their faces,
something that seemed to know all primal secrets, that
made one eager to question them, and yet something
that stilled every question on the lips.

Here and there a group of visitors, men, women
and children, would stop before the parrots, timidly
offering them sunflower seeds and fruit, flirting with
much uncertainty and sudden terror with the brilliant-
colored or white birds whose natures, however alluring,
remained strange and uncanny to them.

"They are tame," thought the curator, "most of them
are perfectly tame. Their chains could be taken off and
they would be just as harmless as they are now." The
recollection of Dr. Wollet flashed through his mind
again. Yes, he might be converted—some day. The curator reflected: "They would fly into the trees if they
were set free, into the zoo. Not one would remain on
its perch. And this avenue of parrots looks so pretty."
He reflected further: "They would frighten the public.

Especially the children. There would be difficulties. No, no, things must remain as they are."

A big, sky-blue macaw, with a dazzling yellow and green top-knot, struggled fiercely with its chain, then laid it carefully and suggestively around its neck. It looked like a clear case of suicide. Suddenly the macaw was dangling, seemed to be lost, if help did not arrive forthwith. Hoarse whistlings, choking gurgles. It rolled its eyes piteously. From all sides people came running, dashing, bounding. Horrified and painfully excited, they gathered around the poor bird, screaming, shouting and roaring for the keeper to come to the rescue. When the hubbub was loud enough, the hanging bird calmly fastened one claw in the chain. A jerk, a lightning-like swing, and the macaw was sitting haughtily on its perch again, looking around contemptuously and screeching like a devil. The curator stood by and smiled. He knew that trick.

He left the shade of the avenue and walked into the bright sunshine where a carpet of flowers bloomed on the broad lawns. Pansies, daisies, forget-me-nots and wallflowers grew against a background of red carnations, running in luxuriant decorative lines across the velvety close-cropped grass. Lilacs, laburnums and jasmines bordered the gay expanse. In the distance a white monument rose from amongst the light and cheerful shrubbery: a little memorial erected to a chimpanzee that had lived here for six years and then died of consumption. Peter's predecessor. He had been called Peter, too. A thought passed through the curator's mind: "And some day the present Peter will die of consumption, too. Perhaps I'll have a monument erected to him. He's earned it, good little Peter has ... And then there'll be another chimp ... and another. ... And in a hundred years there'll be fifteen or twenty stone apes around the garden here." He dismissed the thought and went on.

On the lawns the blackbirds were walking with elegant measured steps, stopping now and again in their search for earthworms. In the shrubbery the finches were chirping, the titmice whispering, the sparrows noisily twittering. Fragrance arose from the flower-beds, from the lilac blossoms, from the freshly sprinkled grass and moist germinating earth. As if for the first time, the curator noticed the long terrace with its many tables, running in front of the restaurant. In the middle distance he saw the pavilion of the orchestra. Not a soul was in sight so early in the morning. The verandah tables were deserted, the music-stands on the pavilion were empty. The curator had little to do with this part of the zoological garden.

On the far side of the lawns were the animals, the zoological garden which had been entrusted to his care for so many years. But, following some compulsion which was not quite clear to him, he was traversing it as if he were a stranger. As far as the imprisoned animals were concerned his conscience was perfectly clear. But he was a sensitive and upright man, and had been somewhat alarmed by Dr. Wollet's remarks and the fate of the mysterious corpse in the elephant house. He was seeking some endorsement of his rule, some reassurance on the whole question of the administration of the zoo.

The high tops of the oaks, elms and plane-trees, the dark foliage of a purple beech towered above the fantastic architecture of the animal houses. A joyful happy life flitted and fluttered through their branches, twittering and singing, screaming and rejoicing in the thick sun-flecked foliage. With delight the curator watched the oriole streak like a winged golden flash from tree to tree. He listened to its melodious piping call. He saw the woodpecker's zigzag flight, heard it pounding on the bark, heard its exultant laugh. He heard a jay's angry rasping from the tree top, and the gentle twittering cry of blackbirds. Then, the furious swift scampering of squirrels passed in a flash of red through the branches.

The curator walked by the cage where the fox was having another of his insane fits, dashing around in a circle. "He's feeling spry," thought the curator, bestowing a sidewise glance on the creature. "Poor fellow, he must have suffered dreadfully when he came to us with that injured foot. I didn't think he'd ever pull through. But now he's recovered completely." He became indignant.

"How stupid and how cruel to set such traps, how piti-less to plan such frightful tortures for poor foxes." He went on, with an agreeable sense of feeling real sympathy for his charges.

He came to the big pond, and affectionately watched the gay population stirring here. Here the denizens of all the zones settled peaceably together. A flock of big gulls from the North Sea fluttered on their clipped wings, a mass of rosy red flamingoes from Africa strutted slowly and elegantly along the turf of the bank. Five or six pelicans, natives of Albania, crouched with philosophic composure at the edge of the water whose mirror-like surface was furrowed by white swans, Chinese ducks, Indian moorhens, lesser divers, and sandpipers from the lagoons of the Adriatic. There were storks and marabus, looking like worried actors and apparently plunged in profound thought. From time to time wild geese waddled ponderously through the grasses, spreading their stumps of wings and uttering their characteristic *cronk,* untamed and unrestrained.

"It is just as if they were free," thought the curator.

"They really are free, and yet they are protected from all danger."

He went on, turning his back on the thwarted flapping of all those clipped wings.

On an enclosed lawn, shaded by lofty chestnut trees, ten or twelve cranes were parading, looking like trim gentlemen in cutaways. They hurried to the wire as soon as they saw the curator. He could not resist their dumb appeals, and slipped into the cage. Then began a strange and solemnly grotesque dance. The curator called the time and the rhythm. The cranes danced around him, keeping step, turning when he turned, sometimes striking at one another with their long breaks. When the dancing man spread his arms, the cranes would flap their abbreviated wings.

"They are happy," he said to himself when he left them, "there is no doubt about it."

He passed the cages where the panther constantly hurled itself against the bars, where the tiger paced restlessly back and forth, where the lion lay in a deep sleep. He passed the bears' den and the monkey house whose hubbub did not detain him. "Delighted as usual," he thought, with a glance at the crowd surrounding the big cage.

He wandered along the gravel walk between the enclosures where were exotic cattle and sheep, strange gigantic or delicate antelopes, tousled, peevish gnus and wild zebras. Many of these creatures, especially among the buffalos and water-bucks, had been born in the zoo, knew no other world beyond this bit of fenced earth and a full manger.

"Happy lives," thought the curator, "happy sheltered lives."

He stood before the cage containing the great birds of prey. The eagle was hulking on the highest tree; carrion-kites, goshawks, sparrow-hawks, falcons and buzzards were flapping up and down with heavy wing-beats. Several owls, big and little hooters, were perched quietly in their stone nook. The curator recalled the time when eagles used to pass their days in cramped cages chained to low posts. He recalled with what long-ing the kingly birds would raise their beautiful eyes to the sky, how they would let their splendid wings droop in order to create that tiny illusion of motion, how their firm hard legs, their sharp talons became soft and feeble, and how the unhappy eagles dropped at last from the perches to which they could cling no longer, and lying on the ground, perished miserably.

"Pillar-saints," the curator had called the unfortunate creatures, thus compelled to suffer all the tortures of captivity. He had obtained the big cage for the birds of prey, had not rested until it was built. Now he stood before it once more as in the first year after its erection, and was filled with the satisfaction of having constructed a paradise for his captives. Of course, the eagles, the goshawks, the falcons, all the princely fowls of the air, could merely flutter within its meshes. The proud flight, on motionless outspread wings, that marvelous circling high up in the region of the clouds, was denied them. In their wings, in their breasts, in their eyes the burning desire for unimpeded flight lived on. Their nostalgia, itself as boundless as space, was granted this miserable enclosure.

The curator turned away.

As he strode slowly between the cages, past the cage which the kangaroos crossed in five or six bounds, past the ostriches that could race around their yard in less than a minute, he made plans, air castles for the animals whom he loved, for whom he would do anything save give them their freedom. He stopped for a moment at the basin where the hippopotamus was standing stupidly in the water, and by the sea-elephant, though the monster never stirred. He watched the seals playing, slithering in sudden short serpentine streaks through the little pool they inhabited.

"Too little room," he thought, "too little room everywhere."

He recalled how he had had to fight for the appropriation for the big bird cage. "Funds," he thought, "funds." If only he had unlimited means at his disposal. What a zoological garden he would build! On a vast terrain that would include whole forests, wide meadows, rocks and big lakes. The gazelles, antelopes, gnus and zebras would live as they do on the open veldt. There would be thickets and clearings for the stags and other deer. The clever seals would swim into imaginary distances, and the beasts of prey, the lions, tigers and panthers, would be given every semblance of freedom.

See them? Oh yes, they would all be seen, that would be taken care of, people would see them as they lived in their natural habitat. And the people would be perfectly safe from them. Some feeble start at such things had been made, at Stellingen, for example. But the curator was dreaming on a fantastic scale.

The idea that wild creatures should not be captured, that the children of the tropics should never be carried into the raw climate of northern lands, that human beings have perpetrated too much cruelty on animals in the course of thousands of years and that it must one day cease—that idea did not occur to the curator.

It would have impugned his own reason for existing. And the curator was very far from doing that.

Chapter Six

Mino Goes Mad

MINO THE FOX HAD GONE quite mad again.

He dashed around his little low cage like a fiend, rushing to the artistic sandstone structure which had been built for him, and then out into the circular barred space through the concrete floor of which ran a drain. In and out. Back and forth.

Stone. Iron bars. Concrete.

It drove Mino mad.

How he hated this travesty of a fox's lair! Whenever he crept into it he recalled his own house which he had built and dug out with his own paws. Yes, that was something different, wonderfully warm and cozy, sunk in the earth of a wooded hill, filled with the movement of life, inside and out, with sprouting and growing things. There had been root fibers and beetles and worms. While he was building it there had even been mice. And what a smell it had! Inside and out. The scent of a thousand victims. Of a thousand dangers. The scent of wife and cubs, trusted and tenderly loved.

Whenever Mino remembered these things a blind rage overpowered him. His blood began to boil and rob him of all his senses.

Often he would lie in the cold, stony, feelingless hole, biting into the walls, spinning around crazily, striking out with all three paws.

For Mino had only three sound paws. A trap had snapped off his fourth. It was the left forepaw. His foot was missing and a bit of the foreleg.

A hunter had found him imprisoned, his leg, maimed by the trap, nearly cut through. Mino was lying flat on the ground, exhausted, almost unconscious from pain and loss of blood, from terror and desperation.

But when the bag was thrown over him, he had rallied all his strength, and bitten and scratched and torn the black, suffocating cover. Lucky for him that he was at the end of his strength. The trapper was thinking of killing him.

But was it really so lucky that Mino had lost consciousness? When he woke up again, there was a heavy chain around his neck. His teeth tore at it in vain till they ached. When the wound on his leg had closed, he was brought here.

He had been here three years now, in this cage. But he had never grown used to it. He could never manage to take it quietly. He never stopped thinking of possible ways of escaping.

It is true that he often lay stretched out all day asleep but this was because he was exhausted by his terrible efforts, his longing.

Sometimes he would sit quietly on his haunches, or lie like a dog on his belly and breast, blinking into space.

Escape.

He laid plans. He would tear up the ground, dig tunnels that would lead him back to the forest. He wondered whether the forest was far or near. And he smiled to himself. Far or near, he would find it. Just let him get outside!

But his feverishly questing nose never found the earth. In his cage there was nothing but stony concrete. His paws ached from constantly scratching at it. It withstood the sharpest, most furious bite he could give.

Then, boiling with impatience, Mino would have one of his insane attacks. Of course he did retain a slight vestige of sense, but it was too feeble to prevent the fit. Mino was raving mad with impatience, with despair, with longing for the death that burns and tortures one.

Inside the hated hole he ran his head against the concrete. A tiny hope flickered through his brain that the fury of his attack would break through the walls. At the same time there was that other hope—that he would break his head and make an end of everything.

Stunned and blinded, he would dash out, rushing around his yard in narrowing circles until he became dizzy and fell down. This dizziness was like freedom to his brain. As far as he could see, the world was spinning round. The bars that caged him spun, and became misty in their mad whirl. The floor turned under Mino's paws. The firm rigidity of the concrete seemed to melt and disappear.

Thus his mad rages helped to change everything. They were the only thing that did help.

To be sure the deception lasted no more than two or three seconds. Then his prison formed around him as firm and immovable as ever. The idea dawned vaguely in Mino's brain that he had not been mad enough.

Furiously he fell upon the bars, bit into the cold iron, pressed his nose, his paws, between the bars so that blood dripped from his jaws, his gums, his pelt.

There was the earth right before him. On the other side of those bars was the earth, naked, trampled by many human feet, softened, and strewn with fine gravel. The earth for which he longed. So near and yet never within reach.

Unhappy Mino raised his injured nose. He caught the scent. The promise of wonderful things was wafted him on the air, to mock, to torture him. There was the piquant scent of pheasants, the enticing scent of rabbits, the sharp odor of the big birds of prey whom the fox believed to be free and reveling in tidbits. Then there was the kindred odor of wolves, of other foxes that made Mino's desire for comrades, for a female companion, intolerable. Oh, how much, how dreadfully much he was deprived of.

Mino flung himself violently away from the bars and began to race about madly again.

A vague, sourish, familiar scent penetrated to him and brought him to a standstill.

There, scarcely a paw's length away, sat Vasta the mouse. She sat outside in the little hole where the drain disappeared in the ground.

Her dark little eyes, like the end of a hatpin, watched the fox. Mino slunk up as if on a mouse hunt. His legs were half crouched and yet tense, ready for a spring, his head lowered and thrust forward. His tail quivered as if it were about to wag.

He stuck his sound paw between the bars and struck at Vasta but could not reach her. Crestfallen, he stood up on his hindlegs, his tail drooping limply, while he gazed innocently out.

"Come to me," he said softly, "come closer."

Vasta sat motionless. She said nothing.

"Come inside," the fox tempted her, "come quickly, come."

"I'll take good care not to do that," said Vasta coolly.

"But I have an important matter to discuss with you," Mino insisted.

"You can discuss it just as well if I remain here. Go ahead, I'm listening."

The mouse sat up; she covered her delicate pointed nose with her two forepaws. "I'd rather go on living," she tittered.

This threw Mino into a white fury.

"Let me out of here!" he snarled. "I want to go on

living too! I, too! That's why I'm dying of grief! Let me out! I've had enough, enough! Do you hear me—enough! Let me out!"

Vasta flitted back into the dark hole before which she had been sitting. "Who—me?" she asked in surprise. "Who—me?"

"Yes, you!" The fox was foaming at the mouth. "Yes, you! You vengeful little beast! You wretched, infamous, good-for-nothing creature! You! Don't deny it! You!"

Vasta sat up as straight as a rod, on her hind-legs, her forepaws lifted in astonishment.

The fox was trembling all over; his eyes had narrowed to little evil slits. "It was you, you and your tribe! It was you that set that monstrous thing to catch me in its iron jaws!" He raised the stump of his forepaw. "The whole forest is filled with you and the likes of you. And all of you are my enemies!"

Vasta laughed. "We—*your* enemies? We?"

"Yes," the fox snorted, "you're small, but you're clever and dangerous! I see now, too late, how dangerous you are!"

"You are mistaken, Mino," said Vasta. But her words were hardly audible for she was proud to be thought so powerful by the fox. She sat up again and took him to task. "Do you admit that you got what you deserved?"

Mino cowered, meek and humble. "I'll admit anything," he whined, "anything you like, anything, anything. Have mercy, have pity on me. You are happy, you are fortunate, you are free. You don't even know how happy, how rich you are. You can go where you want, you can run when you wish. Oh, happy creature! Be kind, be merciful to me! Let me out! I swear I'll never touch one of your race again, never, never! I swear!" He was intoxicated by his own fervent entreaties and a glow of hope. He overshot his promises. "I swear in the name of all my brothers, of all my sisters, never, never more shall one of us harm one of you. We will be friends, good friends. But let me go this time! I swear . . ."

He stopped and gazed out at the empty drain. Vasta had disappeared.

In the distance there was a shout of joy, followed by

savage exultation. A dog—no, Mino knew it was a wolf. He pricked up his ears and listened.

So there was joy here, too! His kinsman was rejoicing. "Only I am suffering," thought Mino, "only I."

Exhausted, he lay down flat on the floor, listening despondently and bitterly. The rejoicings grew softer, then were momentarily renewed, finally died away in silence.

Mino pressed his head between his paws and shut his eyes.

His attack was over.

Chapter Seven

The Wolf and the Law

HUBERT, THE ASSISTANT AT THE zoological garden, had called Frau Marina by telephone. She must come to the zoo as quickly as possible.

Frau Marina was frightened. Had anything happened to her wolf?

"No," the assistant reassured her, "nothing has happened, nothing serious." But she must come right away.

Then why had he called her up? She had intended to visit her wolf today anyway.

"Well," the assistant explained, "the fact is that we don't know what sort of food the wolf is accustomed to. During the three days he's been in the zoo, he's hardly touched a thing we gave him."

"Good Lord!" exclaimed Frau Marina. "The poor fellow; I'll be there directly!"

She lived in a house with a pretty park, in the villa section. Far away in Poland she owned a large wooded estate that often lay deep under snow for months. One day, while she was sleighing through the desolate winter woods, she had come upon a wolf cub in a drift. He was half-frozen, stiff with cold and hunger. She took pity on the helpless little thing, picked him up, rubbed him vigorously, until his whole body was warm, and put him under her fur robe. During the homeward journey she had taken off her glove and put her finger in the wolf's mouth to feel whether he had teeth or not. But all she could feel were fine points as sharp as needles, barely piercing his gums. There was nothing but silken soft lips and a rough little tongue. Lips and tongue instantly began to suckle the warm tips of her fingers.

Frau Marina was quite touched and did not remove her finger until the sleigh reached the manor house. Then she took the foundling into her room, ordered a nursing bottle with warm milk, and fed the young wolf. Prudently. Not too much to begin with.

She recalled that her forester had shot a female wolf several days before. According to his report, she appeared to have whelped recently. That was probably why the forester had also observed she had been so rapacious and daring. He added that now her litter would be sure to die of hunger.

One cub of that litter Frau Marina had found and rescued from starvation. She reflected. The old mother wolf had to feed her children, had to remain strong to suckle them. She must have killed deer, stags and doe after hunting down the poor creatures. She broke into the sheepfold and stole lamb after lamb. What else could she do? She was not to blame, the old mother, regardless of how bloodthirsty she was or appeared to be. But the poor deer, stags and lambs who died with her teeth in their throats were not to blame either. And the forester? Day after day he found the mournful remains of slaughtered deer in the preserve, and bits of murdered lambs. He became enraged at the "enemy" who was causing so much damage. It was his duty to protect the defenseless creatures from the wolf. He could do nothing else, he had to lie in wait, to stalk her and shoot her at sight with a dum-dum bullet that would tear fur, lungs and heart to ribbons. The forester was not to blame. And the young wolves, the helpless cubs who perished miserably of hunger because their mother lay shot in the snow—they certainly were not to blame. Though the children of a wolf, they were children, just as the mother wolf was after all a mother.

With the young wolf in her arms and sucking comfortably at the bottle, Frau Marina gazed out of the window at the forest reposing under its wintry cover.

"The free life of the forest," she thought with a bitter smile.

A sentimental lie! Out there every creature was hunting or hunted. Flight and pursuit, life and death, incessantly, endlessly. Day and night. They were none of them to blame. Those that were killed and those that did the killing. Peace? Was it any different among men? Any better?

Frau Marina forced herself not to let her thoughts stray any further.

The young wolf throve and grew strong. He would not leave Marina's side. If she went out for a few hours, he would whine and howl for a while, then lie down silent with one of her gloves, her wrap or anything else belonging to her that he could steal. They exhaled the scent that quieted him, that lent him patience. He would bury his nose in the bit of leather or wool or cloth, and wait, tense and still. When Marina returned, the wolf would receive her with transports of joy, exulting, flinging himself upon her, doubling up until his head was laughing up at her over his wildly wagging tail, forcing his nose and brow under her hand. At last, proudly and happily, he would fetch her some article in his mouth,

an umbrella, a cushion, a book, as a kind of love-offering;
and in this way his jubilation regularly ended.

He was as obedient to the wave of her hand as the
best of dogs. He guarded her, growled and barked like
a watch-dog, but had never bitten anyone, had never
betrayed by the slightest sign the wildness of his blood.

Frau Marina took him with her to the city. It would
have been impossible to leave him on the estate. He
could not have borne the separation, and with the best
will in the world the people there had not taken very
kindly to him; in general the young wolf's fate would
have been changed in no essential.

When he was a year old that fate was decided.

A police official appeared at Frau Marina's in order
to confirm the rumor that she was harboring a "savage"
animal. Frau Marina received the official politely. He
sat in the drawing-room, and even as he asked the question, carelessly stroked the young wolf who wagged his
tail and rubbed against the official knees.

Frau Marina smiled, indicating the wolf. "There you
have the 'savage' beast."

The official drew back his hand in fright. A silence ensued during which the official regarded the wolf with a rather nonplussed expression.

"You see he is perfectly tame," said Frau Marina at last.

"To be sure, quite tame," the official stammered. "I see he's quite tame . . . ha ha ha!" He laughed in embarrassment and louder than was necessary. "Ha ha . . . that's really quite good—I thought he was a dog, just an ordinary shepherd. Comical, isn't it? So he's really a wolf?"

"If you will examine him more closely," Frau Marina suggested.

"Yes. Well . . . I see. Yes, of course. . . ." The official had recovered his assurance. "Well, tame or not," he said, "the law's the law, my dear lady."

Frau Marina glanced up. "What am I to understand by that?" She was very much disturbed.

"It's quite simple," the official continued, "the animal must be shot, or . . ."

"Or?" She had started violently.

"Or he must be sent to a zoological garden," was the answer.

"And suppose I refuse?" She had risen abruptly and stood prepared for resistance.

The official smiled, and in his furtive, subaltern smile lay all officialdom's superiority. "Then you will pay a fine, madam, assuming that you do not attempt actively to hinder the knacker in the performance of his office. In that case, of course, you might . . ."

"What is a knacker?" Marina exclaimed in fear.

". . . might be sentenced to a term in prison," the official concluded. As if he were now prepared to consider Marina's question, he explained, "The knacker is the official whose function it is to destroy the animals committed to his custody for that purpose."

"Ah!" It was a little cry of indignation.

The official shrugged his shoulders. "The law, madam."

"A very stupid law!" cried Marina, vexed.

"The law," came the reply in a pedantic tone, "is never stupid. At present your wolf is tame, I concede."

"You can't deny it!" Marina interrupted.

"As I said, I concede," the official nodded his head with demonstrative forbearance. "But nobody knows when the wild beast will awaken in him."

"I am willing to guarantee that it never will," declared Marina solemnly.

"The law does not accept guarantees, the law demands obedience." He was fairly bursting with omniscience. Marina fought for her wolf as one fights for a beloved child. She felt that it was a hopeless battle, but she meant to leave nothing untried.

If she took the wolf away, to her estate, he would be out of the country and safe.

Head-shakings on the part of the official. No matter what city in Europe she went to, the law would be relatively the same. Had she not heard of the fad for lions?

No, Marina had heard of no fad for lions. She did not follow fads. This matter of her wolf was something quite different.

"Possibly," said the official. "The fad for lions arose because every year so many young lions are born in the zoological gardens. What is to be done with all these lions? Now there are wealthy people with castles and parks who are glad to buy young lions. Why not? Lion cubs are delightful; they are comical, graceful and as tame as tabby-cats. Only, a little bigger."

He laughed.

"And then?" Marina demanded.

He laughed again. "And then, when the young lions are a year old . . ."

"Well?"

"Well—then they come under the law!"

"You mean they kill them?" Marina cried. "Impossible! Splendid young lions in the very pride of their strength! Impossible!"

"But," the official rubbed his hands, "it is just on account of their strength that they have to be killed. Just on that account! Of course, a circus occasionally takes on a young lion. But not very often. There are too many of them."

Marina resisted no further. She reached an understanding with the official that her wolf should be sent to the zoological garden.

"The first thing in the morning?"

She agreed. At last the official departed. At last Frau
Marina could cry and caress her wolf, the tears running
down her cheeks.

She drove into town at once, had herself announced
to the curator of the zoological garden, and offered to
donate her wolf to the zoo.

The curator thanked her and declined. He had two
wolves. That was enough. His budget did not permit
him to keep more.

Marina had to beseech him, had to relate the whole
story of the wolf, had to describe his gentle, affectionate
nature. She could not restrain a sob as she told it. At
this the curator was touched and promised the wolf an
asylum.

The wolf's arrival at the zoological garden the next
day was somewhat pitiful. Marina had hoped that he
would be received honorably as a welcome gift. That
would have been some slender comfort and have less-
ened the pain of parting. But he was taken in merely
out of pity, like a beggar at an alms-house. She thanked

the curator effusively because her wolf was allowed a cage to himself.

The curator smiled. "The other two wolves are mates. It would lead to fighting."

It was a small cage with strong bars, permitting him to take only a few steps. There was straw on the floor of the dark little sleeping compartment in the rear.

According to the agreement Marina arrived with the wolf in the evening after the visitors had left the zoo. Accompanied by the curator and a keeper, Marina walked toward the cage. The wolf bounded ahead. He was still free. The manifold biting scents that thronged his nostrils from all directions, the calls of the captive animals, their lowing, moaning and groaning, confused him. He sprang back and forth, stopping and wagging his tail in bewilderment. He uttered short barks, running on and stopping again, his eyes fastened questioningly on Marina.

The door of the cage was wide open.

"How are we going to get him in?" asked the curator.

Marina took off her glove. She trembled as she did

so. "Wolf!" she cried, and her voice, with its assumed gaiety, trembled too. "Go fetch it, Wolf!"

She threw the glove into the cage. Wolf bounded in. The keeper slammed the door and bolted it.

"Come, quickly," ordered the curator.

Marina ran so fast that the others could scarcely keep up with her.

Wolf picked up the glove in his mouth and stood for a few moments, perplexed, staring after the departing figures. Then he ran along the bars, seeking a way out.

He thought it was all a game. He did not for a moment dream that he was deserted, that he was imprisoned.

He kept bounding back and forth along the bars, looking for a way out. His nostrils twitched and reassured him with the scent from the glove. His mistress' beloved scent.

Not until Marina was outside on the street, about to enter her automobile, did she hear a high clear loud yelp calling her. She alone detected its trustingly joyful and impatient tone; she alone knew him.

"My poor good Wolf!" she murmured as the automobile bore her away.

Three days had passed. She had not visited the zoo, for by the terms of her agreement with the curator, the wolf must have time in which to accustom himself somewhat to his new home, to his new way of life; must grow tired of howling for his mistress.

"If it was only the howling, madam," said the assistant who was awaiting Marina, "we would never have called you."

"Does he cry very much?" Marina inquired.

"Well—enough," said the assistant. "We're used to that and it doesn't bother us. Of course the public have been pestering the keepers because they all think the wolf must be sick or suffering pain of some kind." The assistant was quite talkative. "Anyway, he seemed to quiet down today. But then he's probably a little worn out and weak by now. He hasn't eaten a bite here yet. Tell me, madam, what did you feed the beast? We've given him everything we could think of. Beef, pork, mutton, liver. He won't eat a thing."

"Raw?"

"I don't understand."

"I mean, was the meat uncooked?" asked Marina.

"Of course," the assistant protested solemnly.

In spite of her despondent mood, Marina could not restrain a smile. "That explains everything! You forget," she said, not without a trace of irony, "that this wolf is a savage beast only in the eyes of the law. I have everything necessary with me."

A loud wailing reached her ears, a mournful plaint that died out in a low whimper. She turned a corner of the walk and saw the cage in the distance. The captive was sitting in the middle, howling out his unhappiness, his head pointed at the sky.

"Wolf!" cried Marina. "Wolf!" She was going to call, "Come here!" But she bit her lip.

Wolf's ears flew up at the first call. At the second he sprang to his feet as if touched by a live wire.

"Wolf!" Marina called again.

Then he saw her, saw her coming nearer. He threw himself against the bars, rejoicing with a deep, ringing bark that broke into a high note. He wagged his tail madly, contorting his body in an ecstasy of bliss, rolling his eyes, laughing and crying at once. And every gurgling, howling, jubilant bark, every movement, every contortion said but one thing—"At last, at last, you have come!"

Marina turned to her chauffeur who was following her. "Let me have it." He was holding a tray.

"The food?"

"Of course."

"Don't you give it to him, please," said the assistant. "Let the keeper feed him." He replied to Marina's inquiring glance with, "He must get to trust him."

Meanwhile the wolf was standing pressed against the bars of his cage, singing his gentle impatience in high, long-drawn cadences.

The keeper took the two dishes.

"What do they contain?" asked the assistant and raised the cover curiously.

"Milk," said Marina with a laugh, "milk in one, and boiled rice with a little meat and marrow bones in the other."

The assistant managed a feeble smile. "Do you call that food for a wolf? We certainly never thought of that. We'd have a hard time providing him with that every day."

They finally decided that Marina should pay for the food.

Then she was permitted to enter the narrow enclosure that separated visitors from the bars of the cage. She stretched both hands between the bars. Wolf stood on his hindlegs, and managed to put his forepaws on her shoulders. He tried to reach her face with his lapping tongue. Marina held his head firmly.

"Be brave, old fellow," she said. "Resign yourself as I've resigned myself. Be brave, be patient, it is only half as bad as death."

The keeper pushed the dishes into the cage, cautiously, as one gives food to wild animals.

Marina pushed the wolf away from her gently. "Eat," she begged, "eat your food!"

Famished, the wolf leaped on his rice, but he kept careful watch and when Marina took a step away from the bars or merely moved, he rushed over to her.

People had gathered and were staring curiously.

Marina waited until Wolf had eaten everything. He came and stood by her. She scratched his head between his ears. "Be brave," she whispered, "goodbye, I'll come again!"

As she released herself from him, he began to howl. She turned to him at once. "Be still, Wolf," she commanded. "Take care of this!" She threw him another glove. "Take good care of it!"

The wolf lay down and put his head on the glove, with intense gravity, duty-bound, and was silent.

Marina left. The wall of people cut her off immediately from his view.

Chapter Eight

Homecoming

MIBBEL LAY STRETCHED OUT peaceably in his cage. He was lying on his left side, blinking indifferently out into the zoo where human faces loitered at the bars or sauntered past. Sometimes Mibbel fell asleep, sometimes he woke up, or was awakened by a human voice, a call, or by moaning roars from one of his kinsfolk in the neighboring cages. Then he would long for Hella, his mate.

When would he see her again, nestling awake or asleep against her soft warm flanks? Why did they keep him from her? He was happy in her company, and would certainly not harm his little sons.

That Hella had two little sons he had heard some time before from Vasta, the mouse.

Why did they separate him from his own kin? He could not understand it at all. Nor did he understand those two-legged creatures in whose power his whole life had been spent.

His thoughts had so often followed this closed circle, a hundred times a day, and they were following it again as he lay there. Everything grew a little hazy, and he fell asleep.

Vasta had been there the first thing that morning to tell him the news.

In the winter cage, she reported, there was a big box with something alive in it. They had just brought it in.

Mibbel recollected that he had heard all kinds of noises behind the partition that divided the summer from the winter cage. But he felt no curiosity either then or upon hearing Vasta's story. He no longer gave it a thought.

But he bounded into the air when the trapdoor rattled behind him, and Brosso trotted leisurely in.

An imposing and terrifying sight was Brosso.

He had a huge flowing mane the dark brown locks of which were tinged with black. His head was held high, his proud and handsome face was distorted and horribly disfigured. In place of his right eye there was a big bloody gash, and the tears that constantly trickled down from it had wet the fine thick hairs on his face far down his cheek, so that they were black and clotted with blood and seemed to exaggerate his injury. The eye itself was closed. But at long intervals the lids would disclose a narrow slit, between which the amber-yellow pupils gleamed.

Brosso walked slowly with the superior mien of the king of beasts. Yet the way in which he set down his feet was full of unutterably impotent sorrow. His gait lacked a lion's springy grace, his joints seemed worn out, his muscles languid and all but flabby.

Brosso wandered once around the cage, his head

held high as when he came in. He made the same round a second time, his head lowered, his nose thrust forward, sniffing and investigating his new quarters. Then he stopped in the middle, lashing his flanks feebly with the tassel of his tail and muttering as if he were quite alone, "What next? What next?"

Mibbel had sinuously avoided Brosso as he paraded the cage, but he never took his eyes off him. Overwhelmed and frightened, at first by Brosso's august appearance, then by distrust and secret anxiety, he prepared to defend himself. But in the end he took a sudden liking to Brosso.

Presently Mibbel advanced with the rolling gait of playfulness, and, lifting his paw, tapped Brosso in fun on the shoulder.

"Stop that," growled Brosso in a tone of command, but without turning his head. Mibbel bounded timidly back.

"Stop it," repeated Brosso more gently.

Mibbel threw himself full length on the floor. "Where did you come from?" he purred.

For a long time there was no answer. At last Brosso deigned to reply, but it sounded as if he were talking to himself. "I am sick. Very sick, indeed. Or is it rest that I need? Yes, yes, rest, rest, rest!" He peered intently into the zoological garden, turning his majestic head to the right and left, while the golden pupil of his right eye flashed as he stared around the cage. "How can it be? I must have been here before. Remarkable! Long ago, very long ago! But I must certainly have been here!"

"I've lived here ever since I was born," said Mibbel, "and I never set eyes on you before."

Brosso's lips twitched scornfully. "Since you were born! Indeed! A young cub like you. . . ."

Mibbel crept closer. "What's the matter with your eye?"

"I should have known it," muttered Brosso. "After all that time I should have known. And I did know it, but . . ."

"You knew what?" asked Mibbel.

"That it was useless," Brosso snorted. "But one always wants to, oh, how dreadfully one wants to. In the end I could think of nothing else. Waking or sleeping, it was always on my mind. At last one can hesitate no longer, one acts whether it means death or not. . . ."

"I don't understand," Mibbel interrupted.

"I leaped at him three times," Brosso continued, "three times, and each time his whip caught me in the eye. Each time, three times, one after the other. . . ."

"I don't understand you at all," Mibbel repeated.

"Didn't they drive you through a long tunnel?" asked Brosso.

"What for?"

"Into an enormously big barred room?"

Mibbel looked his astonishment.

"Sometimes hundreds of those two-legged beasts are sitting outside in a circle. At other times it is all empty. . . ."

"Go on!" urged Mibbel.

"You've never been through it?" asked Brosso.

Mibbel shook his head. "I don't understand you."

With a discreet stroke of his paw Brosso rubbed his injured eye and cheek. "It hardly bothers me," he said, "but I have difficulty in seeing. Not that it makes any difference! That two-legged beast! If I had caught him . . . But the whip cut so terribly! It was impossible. But if I had caught him!" He lowered his head and roared. It was so thunderous, so wrathful, and Brosso roared so long, that presently the other lions, tigers and panthers began too.

Mibbel sprang to his feet, and standing beside Brosso, with his head lowered, roared too with might and main.

But there was no rage in his roar, nor in the roaring of the others—merely grumbling and noise. In Brosso's roar alone was that vengeful white-hot anger, the result of his bitter experience. His roars resounded with primal power above those of all the rest.

Suddenly Mibbel stopped roaring, and pushing Brosso's side gently with his forehead, whispered, "You're out of your mind!"

Mibbel noticed with pity that Brosso swayed at the slight push. He observed also that his new companion had lost a lower fang.

Gradually Brosso quieted down. He had to stretch out on the floor.

"Have you never had to hop up on a narrow little thing," he asked after a pause, "where there's no room to sit, much less to stand?"

"Never!" Mibbel declared solemnly.

"And yet you have to sit and stand. Then the hoops! Sometimes they're burning, sometimes they're covered with paper. But in any case you have to jump through. Through the hoop—it cuts of course. Or through the fire. That singes your hair and makes it smell."

A shudder passed over his back and flanks. He was trembling with indignation.

"I can't imagine why the two-legged beasts are so crazy about such things, or why they torment us so. They have their dogs to do such tricks! That tribe even enjoys doing them. I can't understand that either!"

Mibbel sat quite perplexed. "I have never heard of such things before," he said shyly.

Brosso stared at him. "No? That's good news to me. Perhaps I'll find some rest here at last. And it certainly does you no harm to hear them. Who knows but they may be coming for you tomorrow?"

He pricked up his ears and his tail began to beat the floor. "They're coming now," he growled.

With a supple cowering spring, Mibbel fled to the farthest corner and lay down, pressing himself in mortal fear against the wall.

The curator, an assistant and a keeper appeared. Not to fetch Mibbel, however. They needed him for breeding purposes and had no thought of selling him to a circus. They merely wanted to examine the old lion.

"Hello, old fellow," called the curator, "do you still know me, eh?"

But Brosso did not recognize him. He had traveled about the world for twelve years with the circus. He had a hazy recollection of the zoological garden, but of nothing else. Those twelve years had changed a feeling of indifference and strangeness toward humankind into a feeling of bitter hatred.

He lashed his tail wildly, snarling furiously at the

three men as he trotted back and forth, pushing with his head against the bars.

The curator watched him for a while.

"Shall we call a doctor?" asked the assistant. "His eye seems in a bad way."

"Let it be," the curator decided. "The eye will either heal of itself or he'll lose it. It makes no difference. I don't want to torment the old fellow any further. See how nervous he is."

"Perhaps it is the pain that excites him," the assistant suggested.

"No," said the curator, and the keeper smiled agreement. "His pain is from quite a different cause. He is weighed down by the memory of the circus years, the hard, hard years!" He turned to the lion. "They certainly gave you wonderful treatment. Well, I'll give you your old age pension. God knows you've earned it."

As if in answer Brosso roared, a single short moaning roar.

"Yes, yes, I know all about it," the curator pacified him. "All I need do is look at you, and I know enough!

There, there, it's all right now, old boy." The curator continued to speak softly to the lion who seemed to grow more and more furious. "But don't do anything to my Jackie!" The curator meant Mibbel whom he noticed in the background, anxiously pressed against the wall. "Do you understand? He's not to blame, and can't help your bad temper."

Brosso never stopped pushing his mighty head to the right and left against the bars with angry growls and snarls.

"Let us go," said the curator. "Listen, Gruber," he added to the keeper, "see that the old fellow gets good soft meat, few bones and only such as he can chew up. You'll notice he's lost a fang. He's really in pretty bad shape. But patience, patience! No rough work, I know you understand! He's been beaten enough."

"But everybody says that wild animals are no longer mistreated in training." The assistant remarked.

"Very likely," replied the curator. "That is undoubtedly the truth. But there are wild animals and wild animals. Some are tractable, some obstinate, some gentle, some incorrigible. Some become almost tame, almost! Others never will be. What is a manager to do who has paid a high price for such an animal? The trainer drives it perfectly frantic. For after all, a real trainer is a rare phenomenon. The usual type must simply content himself with browbeating the refractory animal more than the others. . . ."

"Of course," said the assistant, "but browbeating and mistreating are different matters."

"You don't say!" laughed the curator and pointed to Brosso's cage. "You'd better ask the old veteran in there what his opinion is. If he could but talk, he would unfold a tale of pointed iron prods, whips and blank cartridges. He's had his fair share."

They were leaving the cage in the distance.

"For the rest," added the curator, "the old fellow owes the simple fact that he's still alive to his shrewdness or his cowardice—or both."

Chapter Nine

Three Lions Visit the City

BROSSO WAS ONCE IN REAL DANGER. (The curator began his story.) Never before had he been in such great danger.

The circus arrived at Bitterstadt and was to open the following day.

The greater part of the animals had made their solemn entry. It is the simplest and cheapest way to transport animals from the depot to the tents. And the publicity doesn't cost a cent.

You are familiar with such parades, no doubt?

The circus-horses are led or ridden. Then come the work-horses, donkeys and mules. Then the camels and elephants, and perhaps a pair of good-natured feeble bears, with a chain through the ring in their nose. Then the wagon with the monkeys and various harmless smaller animals.

The lions, tigers, panthers and other really wild animals are transported from the depot to the circus at night.

You probably know that these animals travel in cage-like boxes. It is not very comfortable, but there is no better pullman service for such gentry.

At first they are enraged at their cramped quarters. Later, of course, after an all-day and all-night jolting, they become exhausted and quite submissive. Just recollect how such animals come to us after a somewhat longer journey, how tame and broken-spirited they are from exhaustion.

On this occasion they loaded the boxes of lions on a truck. The driver seems to have been a somewhat meddlesome youth. At least so they say. I have no way of confirming it, but no matter how stupidly or recklessly he may have driven, he is by no means entirely to blame, as the circus people would have us believe. For animal boxes must be able to stand anything. Anything at all! That is the first requirement of any box for a traveling circus.

Very well, the driver was doing sixty. Perhaps it was a habit, perhaps his passengers were not entirely agreeable to him. At some point in the city where the streets are narrow and crooked, he made too sharp a turn at a corner. The truck went over the curb.

Rrrmpp! The box crashed down on the pavement.

Crack! A side came off.

In a flash three lions tumbled out on the street.

Escaped!

Oh, I can see it all as if I had been there myself. (The curator sighed.) It's a pity that I wasn't there, the affair would have ended differently if I had been.

Picture to yourself a city street at night, lighted by

arc-lamps. Practically deserted. And in the middle of the road three lions—rolling around, then jumping up, bewildered, terrified and blinking about in amazement, like strangers who do not know just where they should go.

Three enormous lions, wobbling, venturing a few timid steps.

Believe me, I'd have driven them back into that cage with very little trouble. No particular heroism would have been necessary, just a little presence of mind.

Well, a policeman came running up. Naturally, he had had very little experience with lions. He saw the three huge beasts standing together. Rather an uncommon sight, I'll grant that. The policeman was terribly astonished, terribly frightened, but didn't want to show the white feather.

He drew his revolver and fired.

What he thought he was doing, God only knows. Certainly the policeman himself didn't. At any rate, he fired, twice, three times, obviously from much too great a distance. He hit nothing.

Obviously, too, he produced an effect which, while entirely desirable when employed against a mob, was quite the contrary in the case of three lions. The moment the shots were fired, the lions did just what the mob would do—turned tail and scattered.

With that the evil was done.

Each of the three took a different direction. Each carried the terror of his presence into another locality. The panic spread, tripled, quadrupled, throughout the city.

What would you expect, my friends? When face to face with animals, human beings are incredibly stupid. Especially when face to face with an animal that can defend itself. In the case of an animal that is reputed to be kingly, savage, ferocious, people are not only stupid, they are pitiable cowards.

And note well, there is no more dangerous, no crueler beast on earth than a stupid, cowardly man.

Three poor lions! They were much more frightened than all the people in the city put together. The people knew where to find refuge. The people were not pursued and not attacked. But they thought they were.

The three lions were terrified by their sudden freedom. The crackle of shots sent a thrill of fear through their bones. In the stony world of the city they did not know what to do. They did not know what to do in the world in any case. They were perfectly helpless and had only one mad desire—to be locked up in safety. They were accustomed to that from their birth.

Though lions sometimes turn savagely on their trainer, in their first moment of undesired freedom, there is not a trace of viciousness or wildness in them. They are bewildered, frightened and as easy to manage as children. Of course, later on, after they've been hunted and driven to desperation they are capable of fierceness. I'm not denying that in any way. But this time matters did not take that course. The lions were left no time for that.

The unfortunates showed from their manner how fervently they longed for some cubby-hole, some cage in which to hide.

One of them ran after a bus and caught it when it

stopped. Obviously thinking that here was a safe haven, he crept eagerly in. The bus contained a single passenger, a fat and elderly wine-merchant. He simply froze stiff with horror when the lion suddenly entered, so stiff that he forgot to rub his eyes.

Choking with terror he could do no more than gargle a brief groan. Then he threw up the window and with one plunge was in the street. Since his schooldays the man had never taken such a header. But necessity is the mother of gymnastics, even in the case of a fat and elderly wine-merchant. He was convinced that the lion had boarded the bus with the sole intention of seeking him out and devouring him. Therefore he hurled himself from the window and ran for all he was worth. The driver and conductor were already in flight. The bus was deserted.

Inside, however, the lion crouched in the narrow aisle, waiting. He was still so frightened that his tongue hung out and his flanks heaved from his soft panting.

But he lay quite still and remained perfectly peaceable.

The second lion trotted past the houses for a while, looking everywhere for some spot to hide. At last he found an open door and scampered in. It was the Hotel Ritz!

His reception was not wholeheartedly enthusiastic.

In a flash the elevator boys headed the cars skywards without waiting for the doorman or an official who attempted to crowd on. Even the most robust and impudent lackeys galloped away in mad flight, like hunted antelopes.

Within the space of two seconds the lower hall was swept bare of human life, while the night-clerk barricaded himself in a telephone booth and sent the alarm to the police.

Meanwhile the homeless lion was snuffling about the lobby. He lay down on the thick carpet but did not feel at ease. The room seemed too wide, too open. He rose, discovered the gloomy stairs and scampered up. He bounded aloft as if he had a most painful sensation of invisible foes in full pursuit.

He ran to the fifth floor. There the narrow corridor tempted him. He slunk along it, hesitantly, with a worried expression like someone who has lost his way.

You know, my friends, that by nature lions are very peaceable and timid. You know, too, that only danger, a threat or a wound can arouse the full force of their terrible rage.

I am willing to guarantee that never was a lion so peaceably inclined, so timid or so meek as the poor fellow who settled down outside that fifth floor door.

Incidentally, the door seemed familiar; it looked like the entrance to a cage. So he crept into the deep frame, settling into its accustomed narrowness. He pressed his nose against the latch, waiting for some keeper to open up for him.

And indeed the door was opened for a moment. The tiniest little crack. The gentleman who was passing the night in the room wished to set his shoes outside.

Right under his nose he beheld the massive head and flowing mane of the lion. The two stared eye to eye, man and lion. Both surprised, both bewildered. But

I would like to wager that it was the man who was the more hateful and exasperated at that moment, the more ready, in his terror, for any cruelty.

I admit that it is only rarely that one opens the door of one's hotel room to find a lion waiting outside, apparently desirous of entering. I admit that the gentleman who was about to set his shoes in the hall and thereby nearly came into collision with a real live lion on the fifth floor of a Central European hotel is probably the first and only person to whom such a thing ever happened. He slammed the door, turned the key and even shot the bolt. Understandable enough. A solid citizen who wants to go to sleep and comes to the door in his underdrawers and slippers is neither in the humor nor qualified to settle conclusions with a lion. But how absurd it becomes when he rushes to his telephone and roars at the clerk, "What kind of a management is this?"

The third lion had the worst luck. He strayed onto a dance floor. Slinking past the horrified doorman, he spread terror and wild panic in the small overcrowded hall. But he was himself certainly the most terrified, the most panic-stricken.

The jazz suddenly broke off on a plaintive note. The dancing couples crashed screaming into one another, or sought refuge on the orchestra's platform, or sought exits. All around the empty dance floor, against the walls, and in the loges, pale and tottering gentlemen and deathly white, shrieking, weeping, wailing young ladies pushed and pressed.

The lion stood trembling in the middle of the dance floor—which was slippery. He gazed around in desperation.

Several of the ladies sprang upon tables and held up their skirts, screaming as if they beheld a mouse. Glasses fell with a crash to the ground.

At the sound the lion shrank together.

Somebody threw a champagne bottle at him. In an instant dozens of champagne bottles were flying through the air, some of which reached their mark. The hail of bottles made a sound of thunder.

This bombardment, together with the hellish uproar and the bottles that took effect, combined to render the lion mad with fear. Crouching, he strove to find some shelter, some salvation, and spying the dark opening of a loge, he sprang with one enormous bound over tables and bombardment and howling humanity, toward the sheltering corner.

For all he cared, everybody could leave the place quietly and at his leisure. He had found his nook, where he proceeded to lie down, breathing heavily, his nerves aquiver, his pulses pounding: he wanted peace and quiet.

When the uproar which had been caused by the general brainless pell-mell flight had died down, calm was restored. By that time the police had arrived—at the bus, the hotel and dance hall.

They might have heeded the tearful entreaties of the circus director, the trainer and the keepers, they might have afforded them every opportunity to recapture the fugitives. It might have been a sufficient fulfillment of their duty simply to stand guard over the lions with guns ready and wait to see whether any of them were savage.

But the police had guns, they were men summoned "to restore order," and they did not hesitate a moment. Perhaps, too, since none of them had ever shot a lion in his life, this seemed a more favorable moment than was ever likely to present itself again.

Enough, all three patrols acted in the same fashion. Riddled by their bullets, the lion in the bus fell dead.

The lion on the fifth floor of the Hotel Ritz they laid low in the W.C. whither he had fled, mortally wounded.

The third lion perished under their murderous fire in that charming nook which he refused to abandon.

Now you see why I say that old fellow we have with us was very cunning. Doubtless you observed that he can be savage on occasion?

But that night he did the most cunning thing it is possible to conceive. He simply remained in the broken box. He did not as much as poke out his nose. He stretched out as far back as he could get, and appeared to be asleep. He did not disturb the circus people when they came and again nailed up the box.

That is how he saved himself. A sly fellow!

When the director of the circus asked me if I would accept the old rascal, I gladly agreed. There you have Brosso's story.

Chapter Ten

Peace Pact

PETER THE CHIMPANZEE WAS RIDING his bicycle through the zoological garden, Eliza, as usual, walking beside him.

It was still early morning and there were few visitors, though several elderly ladies and gentlemen were strolling along the walks, a few students were roaming about, with now and again a pair of lovers whose interest in the animals was nominal. In the wide park, governesses, nurses and young mothers were seated on the benches, their baby-carriages in front of them, supervising the sleep of their charges which, in the mild sunshine, were acquiring cheeks the color of pears. In the sand pile were playing the little children who did not have to go to school yet and could pass the whole day in the open. The soft hum that was made up of the chatter of women and the clear voices of children was shattered now and again by the roar of some beast of prey, the croak of a bird or the screeching of monkeys. Nobody paid any attention to such interruptions.

Presently the soft patter of conversation turned into a joyful and delighted surprise.

Peter was passing by.

The children jumped up, and ran for a short way beside Peter, eager to guide his bicycle for him. Several loiterers stopped to gaze with amusement at the noisy little swarm at whose head the grotesque and exotic cyclist was playing his pranks. Then the children gave up following him.

Once more Peter was alone with Eliza.

He was perched on the kind of low bicycle that is

made for small children. He rode very slowly, for he had long ago observed that Eliza could only keep up a certain pace.

The fine gravel crunched softly under the smoothly rolling tires.

But sometimes Peter would pedal fast and shoot away like an arrow. Eliza walked on undisturbed. She knew Peter's delicate consideration.

And she was right. After his short spurt, Peter would make an easy and elegant turn and come back, would turn again gracefully, or at any rate artistically, and be at Eliza's side once more.

He watched her good-naturedly out of affectionate and thoughtful eyes—eyes in whose depths there was always a heavy sorrow. His was the grave expression of an aged man whose face is furrowed and creased with a thousand experiences, sorrows and secrets. He pursed and puckered up his ugly protruding lips, childishly, soliciting, demanding attention.

"Yes, that's a fine fellow," whispered Eliza, "a good Peter."

He took his hand from the handle-bars, and laying it on Eliza's shoulder, glided along beside her with an appearance of perfect contentment, as if to say, "Everything in order."

Of course, this was not the usual hour for his bicycle ride. Usually Peter rode along the walks in the afternoon when many people had gathered in the zoo. He always wore some kind of fantastic uniform, and a whole crowd of children and grown-ups would follow him everywhere, laughing, howling and shouting. These processions were among Peter's great triumphs. At these moments he was the success, the sensation of the whole zoo.

As he rode about, followed and surrounded by a vast train that yelled and shouted and tried to play him all kinds of tricks, he was the only creature whose manner was quiet and dignified.

But his features, apparently so ancient and so candid, beamed with gratification.

That day Peter had fetched his bicycle in the morning and with all the stormy, stubborn insistence of which he was capable on occasion, demanded to be taken riding. He knew to a second the time appointed for his outing but he felt a sudden desire to go at once. It was one of his whims, and Eliza found no good reason not to grant it. The sky was clear and blue, the air was motionless, the sun warm, almost hot. As the sparkling cascade of the sprinkler passed by, a fresh smell arose from the grass and flowers.

Presently he removed his hand from Eliza's shoulder, his feet pedaled faster, and he was off.

Suddenly he stopped and sprang to the ground. Flinging the bicycle down carelessly, he hurried to a cage.

Eliza walked faster.

A stag had noticed the monkey riding a bicycle and had come bounding up in alarm to the wire fence. A big red stag whose huge dark-brown antlers were tipped with shiny white.

Peter saw the menacing, onrushing stag. This unfamiliar sight made him desert his bicycle and forget everything else. His curiosity was at fever pitch. In a flash he had rushed to the cage.

The stag too was curious, not to say suspicious.

When Peter inserted his arm through the wire to stroke or to seize the stranger, the stag lowered his head with a sudden twist, and a hard blow from one of his antlers caught the chimpanzee's limb.

Peter quickly drew back. That hurt! For a second he was dumbfounded with pain and surprise. Then his anger blazed up.

He crouched down, beat his knuckles on the ground, uttering his cry of rage—"Oeh! Oeh!"

He seized the bars and scaled them in a twinkling, intending to swing himself over and take vengeance on his foe.

But Eliza, dashing up, caught him by one leg, and ordered him down. Peter resisted a little, and argued with Eliza: "Oeh! Oeh!"

As Eliza would not let go, Peter gave up and climbed down beside her. But he shouted abuse, blasphemous abuse, explaining how much he detested the stag, stating most explicitly how loathsome he considered him, how dreadfully he longed to be able to tear him into little pieces.

The stag stood, threateningly immobile, on the other side of the wire. Majestically he tossed his proud head with its wide-spreading antlers.

Eliza glanced now at him, now at Peter. She laughed. Laughing, she bent down to the little black fellow. As he was not wearing his uniform she could see the thin hair on his skin. "Peter, Peter!" She smiled at him, and stroked his forehead, head and neck to quiet him. She scratched him and slowly Peter grew more calm.

Eliza searched her pocket, and discovering a few nuts, offered one to Peter. "Here—crack that!"

In a twinkling the cracked nut was lying in her hand. She took out the kernel and offered it to the stag. "Eat it! There, there, that's right!"

The stag snuffed her extended hand suspiciously, hesitating, and his soft warm breath again brushed her hand. She laughed. "Eat it. That's right. You'll like it."

Presently the stag's soft moist lips were munching the kernel.

Then he tossed his head again. His big soft eyes asked very simply and eloquently–"Another!"

Eliza made Peter crack another nut. He had watched her offering with curious intentness. Eliza laid the nut in Peter's hand. He started to carry it to his mouth, but she held his wrist.

"Be nice, Peter, and give it to the stag."

Peter wanted to eat the tasty morsel himself; he had not the slightest desire to do his enemy a favor. Eliza guided his hand toward the wire. At first Peter clenched his fingers around the nut.

The stag saw both hands in front of him, the human hand and the monkey's fist. He snuffed at them, wanted to butt them with his sidewise lowered head, but he considered, snuffed again, and as his silken, soft, warm lips brushed over Peter's fingers, the chimpanzee opened his fist as if at a caress. The nut lay, a little the worse for wear, on the palm of his hand, and the delicate lips removed it.

Peter was entranced. Quite like a child, his rage turned to joy, his thirst for vengeance to a grateful affection because his supposed enemy had accepted a gift from him.

In the stormy emotion which now transported him, Peter seized the next few nuts that Eliza handed him, cracked them and offered them joyfully and impetuously.

With a reserve that scarcely betrayed his desire the stag followed every motion that Peter and Eliza made. He stood majestic and almost helplessly timid, eager for the nut, yet still suspicious. He had raised his head with a somewhat equivocal dignity, ready at any moment for offense or defense, but at the same time inclined to accept the tasty tidbits.

For the third time his warm blowy breath snuffed Peter's hand, for the third time Peter felt the agreeable caress of those velvety lips, and gazed three times into the soft shimmering darkness of those glorious eyes.

But when at last he pursed his lips splendidly for an answering kiss, the stag tossed his head wildly and

THE CITY JUNGLE ❧ 141

started back a few steps into the enclosure. His gesture was that of haughty rejection and said—"Enough!" But Peter in his ravishment noticed nothing at all of this unfriendliness. He was making all preparations to clamber up the wire and swing himself over. All that he wanted now was to stay close to his new friend.

Eliza stopped him. "Come, Peter," she said. "Come. Be a good boy! That's enough for today."

Obediently Peter picked up his bicycle and jumped on. As he rode away, he waved one hand to his comrade. It was a childish, careless gesture which, like all those he had learned from human beings, had made but an indistinct impression on Peter's mind.

The stag wheeled about, and walking very stiffly to the corner of his cage, stared after the departing figures. Who was that creature? Accompanied by a human beast, too! But his odor was not human, though otherwise quite strange. Perhaps a captive like himself, and yet free to wander around the zoo. Who was he?

Chapter Eleven

A Fool

HOME AGAIN IN HIS GLASS HOUSE, Peter was overcome by that exhaustion to which at times he was prone.

He rolled listlessly on the floor, and creeping limply to his bed, lay still. His face, his shrewd eyes exhibited a sorrow that was shocking.

The stag, his ride, everything seemed forgotten. Eliza knew these attacks; they filled her with anxiety. She sat rather dejected after the failure of her efforts to interest Peter in some grapes or a piece of orange.

Suddenly she started. An elderly gentleman was standing beside her, saying, "Perhaps you should give Peter a glass of red wine."

She rose. "How did you get in here? It is forbidden."

"Forbidden?" replied the stranger. "Pardon, I did not know that."

Eliza looked at him and she felt less afraid.

The gentleman was dressed entirely in black, there was black crepe on his hat, and on his pale and kindly face a shadow of deep melancholy. Eliza could not recall where she had seen this face.

"No, it is not allowed," she said, but her voice was now mild and somewhat bewildered, "and I must ask you . . ." She hesitated.

The stranger looked at her as if each of her words made him curious.

She began again. "If . . . if everybody were allowed in here, just imagine . . ."

"But my son visited little Peter so often," said the gentleman. He was silent and seemed to be struggling with something that prevented him from speaking. Then Eliza realized that this was Rainer Ribber's father.

Tears came into her eyes and ran down her cheeks. She took her handkerchief and wiped them away, but fresh tears kept welling out.

The gentleman went on speaking. "Rainer loved the little fellow so dearly. . . ."

Eliza was sobbing aloud, crying into her pocket-handkerchief. She could not utter a word.

"He loved all the creatures here in the zoo very dearly," his father continued.

Another silence.

"He loved all creatures everywhere," said his father with a sigh. "Not only the prisoners in here, but those that live outside in freedom." He interrupted himself, repeating with a strange emphasis, "Freedom! But it was these poor captives that possessed his whole heart."

"Oh," cried Eliza, "he was such a dear fellow."

"Even as a little boy," Rainer's father went on,

talking to himself. "We had canaries, but he wouldn't stand for it. Even as a little boy. The idea of keeping a poor little bird in a tiny cage! Rainer would be quite filled with despair when he saw it." He sighed again. "Yes, yes, the child . . . the child. Perhaps he was extravagant in some ways, but I am no longer any judge, for he brought us up, brought up his own parents to feel as he did."

"He was such a nice, likeable lad," said Eliza again, softly.

"He found you, too, extraordinarily sympathetic, Miss Eliza."

Eliza dried her tears and even tried to smile. Rainer's father knew her name. It was almost a kind of bond between them, she felt.

He pointed to the chimpanzee who was asleep in his bed, his hands over his face. It looked as if Peter were pressing back some dull pain or heavy sorrow in order not to suffer unbearably.

"He always pitied that poor little fellow so much. . . ."

"Pitied him?" Eliza would not have contradicted for

anything. "But nobody needs to pity Peter, he gets along very well. He's happy." She waxed enthusiastic.

"Do you think so?" answered Rainer's father. "You are devoted to him, nobody can deny that, and my son thought so much of you—but just look at the little creature now, does he look very happy?"

Eliza glanced at him, and for a moment she was taken aback. "But Peter is asleep," she objected. "You can't really tell. . . ."

"Perhaps you are right," said Rainer's father very slowly, "perhaps, but I am accustomed to accept my son's judgment in such matters. And it seems to me that my son was right. You know, he always used to say that that little sleeper was as disturbing as a hopeless cry."

Then it occurred to Eliza that Rainer had visited the cage that last evening to see Peter asleep. She averted her head.

Beside Peter's bed, Rainer's father was talking in a low voice. "What it is, I don't know, but now I understand my son. I am very close to him now, very close.

An animal like this reveals himself very clearly when he's asleep. It is not as if Peter were grieving at being far from his tropical forest, without brothers or sisters, alone in an artificial existence. He has amusements, of course, he has everything possible. But everything possible is only a substitute and no substitute can ever make up to him for nature."

Eliza's eyes flew open.

"He can't tell you what he lacks, poor speechless Peter," Rainer's father continued, turning to her. "He can't explain it even to himself. But he feels that the most important thing of all is lacking. What I call—I heard it first from my son—the roots of his existence. The nourishing sources of his vital energies are lacking."

Eliza shrugged her shoulders. "Your son was a dear fellow, a very dear fellow, but he was always extravagant."

"You are right!" his father agreed. "You are right! The rest of us always call a soul like Rainer's extravagant." He began to soliloquize. "But everything noble, everything merciful, every liberating force was brought into the world by people who were extravagant just as you were extravagant, my Rainer! Where would the world be today were it not for the people we call extravagant? Can you deny," he asked, touching her arm with a finger she barely felt, "that the premonition of an early death is hovering over this chimpanzee? Can you deny that this chimpanzee has submitted with perfect gentleness, with infinite patience, with a resignation of which few humans would have been capable?"

"What do you mean? An early death? For Peter?"

Rainer's father became harsh. "You know just as well as everybody else that chimpanzees, like other captives, are subject to premature death."

"I'm doing everything," Eliza protested in terror, "everything I can. . . ."

"Nobody questions that," interrupted Rainer's father. "You make a real effort. Of course. So does the curator. So do many of the keepers. Of course they do. But first you capture all these creatures, these innocent unsuspecting helpless creatures. Then you make them suffer the torture of transportation. Then you subject them to the torture of being caged. And after all that, you begin to be kind to them." He laughed, a short sharp laugh. "Oh, this *garden,* this *garden . . .*"

Eliza stared at him bewilderedly. "Good heavens, you mean that this garden should not exist?"

"Oh yes, this garden has to exist! Too many people demand it, declare that it is useful, instructive, a cultural necessity, a joy to young and old! Too many people maintain that! But not I, not I! As for me, I have not even dared say that there never will be any true culture until people no longer find joy in caged animals, there will be no true culture until people no longer think of this garden as a place of enjoyment, but as a place of horror. . . ."

Eliza shrank back. The strange gentle old man, who really did not seem strange to her at all, Rainer's father, seemed to be insane.

He seemed, too, to read this feeling on her face. "No, Eliza," he said, "I am not insane. I did not know the truth about this garden until I wandered through it with my son's farewell letter and recalled his words, which are verified so terribly at every turn."

"A farewell letter?" Eliza trembled.

Rainer's father nodded silently.

"Did he know then . . . ?" she asked, and began to tremble so violently that she had to support herself against the bars of the cage.

Rainer's father bowed his head and was silent for a long time. His head still bowed, he began to speak at last in an infinitely weary voice.

"'Man is tormented and torments the animals.' That is what he wrote in his letter. I know it by heart, I've read it here so many times every day. Oh yes, the letter came, but it was all over by then. . . ." He could not go on.

"Terrible," murmured Eliza.

"Yes indeed!" He raised his voice a little. "'Tis true 'tis terrible, and terrible 'tis true." Then he added the incomprehensible word "Polonius."

"He also wrote: 'Can I say as other men say—*What do*

I care? No, it's impossible!' And he wrote: 'I feel all the sufferings of God's creatures, but all their sufferings are too much for me!' Too much, poor boy, poor dear boy!'" His father was weeping with quiet, strangely dry sobs, that shook his body and forced a kind of twittering whistle from his breast. But presently he recovered his composure. Simply, like a man who has no part in what he relates, though his face was ashen-gray, he continued. "'If none of the beasts of prey will take me,' he wrote, 'and the beasts of prey are unhappy and broken, if none of them will take me, I will go to the elephant. He has a little pet that he protects, and can be made very angry. He is strong.' Yes, those are his words. 'I will give myself to him as a sacrifice, an atonement for everything, for all. . . .'"

"No!" cried Eliza.

"'For everything, for all,'" repeated Rainer's father. He laughed, a soft laugh. "A fool!" nodding emphatically as if in affirmation of his judgment. "Yes, indeed, a fool! A fool whom God has punished! Everybody will say so! That is why the letter must remain secret! Shh! Shh!" He laid his index finger on his pale thin lips. "I'd laugh myself," he tittered, "even I, if he weren't my son." His titter twisted into a stifled sob. "My only son, who made me what I am. . . ."

Without another word he departed.

Chapter Twelve

Father and Son

THE EARLY MORNING SUN ILLUMI-
nated the orangutan's house. The bright
May sun. Strong, warm, bursting buds.

Yppa sat holding Tikki, her baby, at her
breast. The bright light of the sun penetrated to Yppa
with diminished force through the panes in the glazed
roof and walls.

Inside it was warm and humid from the partially
throttled steam. In this way an effort was made to

imitate and find a substitute for the humidity of the jungle. But the empty room, fenced off by solid bars, did not in the least resemble the jungle, and in spite of its size, remained just a narrow cage. The sole effect of the moist air was to prevent Yppa and Tikki from being cold. Otherwise the air which was sealed in had nothing in common with the tropical warmth of their native forests.

But the sun . . . Yes, Yppa recalled a piercing dazzling light, a vast fire which had meant sun to her in days long past. What was this feeble glimmer to her now?

But Yppa no longer noticed the difference. Some sense of it remained in her nerves, pulsed in her blood, shrouded her whole existence. But this feeling itself was now so deeply shrouded that she hardly ever suffered because of it.

She had no thought but for Tikki whom she was holding in her arms. She lived only for Tikki. She was happy that this permitted her to forget the feelings in her heart.

From time to time she thought of Zato, her companion in this cage, her mate, Tikki's father.

He had disappeared during the night on which Tikki had been born.

Yppa guessed that he was close at hand, for in the course of the days and nights she had occasionally caught Zato's scent.

She did not know what had happened to him, and worried about it now and again, but not for long. Her whole attention was centered on the little creature at her breast. But whenever she imagined the meeting between Zato and Tikki she trembled with fear.

At present she was sitting in a careless posture, letting her glance rove dreamily here and there as the baby suckled. Always, when she could feel the little thing's diminutive lips at her breast, she passed into this twilight state and was soothed to the point where she might be said to be happy.

That was Vasta's impression, too. She crouched in the tiny crack where she always sat. Yppa had never yet noticed the mouse nor had Vasta ever ventured to address Yppa.

She was afraid of the mother orang's hands, those

terrible hands that looked so human. She trembled at the sight of those fingers that could grip so cleverly, and would certainly be able to reach into Vasta's crack. But today her dark little beady eyes were fastened curiously on Yppa. Vasta's cobwebby but rigid whiskers vibrated nervously as, at last, summoning all her courage, she finally asked Yppa a question. "Are you happy?"

Yppa had heard apparently, as a slight twitch of her features showed. But she did not answer.

Vasta waited a while. "I saw how you despaired," she whispered. "And I felt so sorry, so terribly sorry for you."

The mother orang fixed her glance on the glass roof as she covered Tikki with her hands. She seemed to hear nothing.

"I watched you so long," the mouse warmed up to her subject. "So long. I know that I am as nothing compared to you, that a blow from your finger could crush me to death, but I felt such pity . . ." She stopped short, terrified.

The inner wall had been pushed back noiselessly.

Zato entered the cage. Huge, powerful, his manner was unfathomable and mysterious.

Yppa did not move.

Even Vasta, who was overpowered by curiosity, did not stir from her place.

The inner door was opened still wider, disappeared in the wall. Once more the entire cage was open to view.

With his arms Zato seized the bare branches of the strong dead tree and swung himself forward until he stood before Yppa. He looked at her. There may have been tenderness in his eyes and manner. Only he himself could know—though perhaps Yppa divined it too.

She did not stir. But she lowered her glance.

Zato sat down in front of her. Perfectly still. He remained in that position for an hour, two hours.

It was too long for restless little Vasta, and she slipped away. She felt somewhat offended, for she had never been so snubbed in all her life.

Zato sat for hours until Yppa gathered courage to look into her mate's eyes. Then she was no longer afraid for Tikki or herself.

They remained thus for a long time, facing each other, deaf to the keeper's allurements, as indifferent to the proffered fruit and tidbits as if they had been blind.

Zato picked up some of the straw that covered the floor and let the wisps slide between his fingers aimlessly.

Yppa did the same, but only with one hand. The other held Tikki. He was asleep.

At last, toward midday, when the house containing their cage was deserted, Zato picked up one of the bananas that had been tossed in and offered it to Yppa with a slow, almost solemn gesture.

Slowly and solemnly Yppa accepted the luscious fruit.

Then Tikki awoke and clambered up on his mother's shoulder, awkward and childish. He turned his old man's face toward Zato and immediately an expression of unbounded astonishment passed over it.

Cautiously Zato reached for him. He took him from his mother who surrendered him quietly. Holding the thin little body reclining in his hands, Zato bent over it and fondled Tikki carefully, but with passionate devotion.

In a few moments Zato got up, holding the little thing in one hand close to his face; with the other he seized a branch and in one enormous swing reached the farther, most distant corner of the cage.

Yppa did not move but her constantly watchful glance followed every step and gesture Zato made.

He sat in his corner turning Tikki round and round at arm's length as one examines a piece of cloth.

This game lasted a long time. Tikki, not understanding it at all, nevertheless seemed not to mind in the least and readily surrendered himself to his father's hands, trusting Zato who again held him close to his face when Tikki stretched his little arms and tried to reach him.

Of course Tikki grew restless after a while. He was hungry and wanted his mother. Zato would not let him go.

Yppa noticed that the little one was hungry. She got up and went to him. Before she could reach him Zato sprang up and swung past her to the other corner of the cage.

His action was perfectly gentle and he showed no sign of ill-temper or anger. But his manner bespoke absolute determination. He did not want to give Tikki back.

For a little while Yppa did not disturb him. Then she approached again. At her very first step Zato changed his place, circled around Yppa and crouched as far away as possible in a corner.

This was repeated several times. The gigantic orangutans kept circling restlessly around their cage, constantly eluding one another. Both perfectly serious, imperturbable, almost solemn.

The afternoon visitors watched these proceedings with amusement and took them for a game of teasing.

Once Tikki looked over Zato's shoulder at Yppa and stretched out his thin little arms to her longingly. Zato covered the little one's head with his soft, powerful hand, hid Tikki in his breast, against his neck and fled into another corner.

Everybody laughed.

"A family idyll," they said.

But it was no idyll.

When by strategem they had succeeded in separating Zato from Yppa the night before the birth, he too had known what hours of pain lay before her. They were closely bound to one another in expectancy, anxiety, fear and hope. Suddenly Zato found himself alone and he was very much upset.

Of one thing he was certain: Yppa had no part in it. One thing he sensed quite clearly, Yppa was just as much in the power of whatever force had brought them here and kept them captive as he.

His spirit was so broken by what he had been through that he felt all resistance to be vain. He had become too timid and weakly to feel rage or anger. Gentle and submissive, he sat all day long alone and waited.

From time to time he believed that all was lost, and that he would never see Yppa again. Then he was plunged in melancholy.

But there were moments, too, when Tikki's soft squeakings reached Zato's listening ear. That encouraged him again and he waited more patiently.

Patience, heroic endless patience never forsook the orangutans.

At last they permitted Zato to enter the big cage again. He went from the small cage where he had been lured and driven and where he was isolated by a partition from Yppa, back into the large cage. The hole that had been closed so long was again opened. Zato immediately slipped through. But then there was that iron door that divided the big cage in two. Zato confronted it, trembling, tense, did not stir from the spot, staring incessantly at the coffee-brown iron surface. Then that pitiless obstacle too disappeared without a trace, and Zato saw Yppa, saw for the first time his son.

Now he had seized him, now he had taken Tikki to himself, now he was filled with just one purpose—come what might, they would never again separate him from Tikki, never again. He would let no one hold Tikki but himself, he would not let him out of his arms for a single moment.

Yppa finally gave up trying to reach Zato directly. She did not for a moment consider an open struggle

with him. She knew that Zato was the stronger. Moreover her instinct told her that Tikki would be in terrible danger if she attempted to seize him by force.

So she began to draw close to Zato very slowly,
hardly perceptibly, as she thought. But Zato saw her.
He always let her approach to within a certain distance
and then by retreating showed her how futile it was.

Yppa sat down and buried her face in her hands in
desperation.

"If only night would come! If only we were alone!"
thought Zato.

But they were not alone.

Twilight settled slowly down and the visitors had to
leave the orangutans' house and the zoo.

Nevertheless Zato and Yppa were still not alone.

The keeper had noticed some time before what was
going on and had already summoned the curator. The
two men were standing in front of the cage.

"Be a nice fellow," the curator coaxed, "be nice,
eh? You're such a nice fellow, aren't you, and you love
your little son so much, don't you? Anybody can see

how much you love him. But just remember that the little one can't live on love. He's hungry. He must go to his mother. Be a nice fellow. Let the baby go to his mother. . . ."

The curator stopped and waited a little while before beginning again. He spoke a long time in a very tender voice.

Zato's distrust increased with every word that he heard but could not understand.

He turned his back on the two men outside the cage, turned his face to the wall in a corner and waited.

"If we could use a noose on the old fellow," began the keeper.

"Impossible!" the curator replied. "He'd injure the young one seriously if he didn't kill him." To the keeper's questioning glance he replied, "Not intentionally, of course. Only in his first struggles, when he felt the noose, or by some accidental twist . . ."

"If we could hold his hands . . ." the keeper began again.

"Can't be done." The curator dismissed it with a wave

of his hand. "It would be all right, if we were sure of succeeding at the first try. But who is going to guarantee me that?"

He walked to the door. "Remove every bit of fruit from the cage and watch carefully while you're doing it, but be quite calm about it, Andreas."

With that he left. Meanwhile Andreas cautiously removed the grapes, oranges and bananas from the straw with a long-handled shovel.

When the curator again visited the orangutans' house, Zato had turned around and sat, leaning against the bars, with Tikki clasped under his chin, apparently plunged in thought. Tikki dangled, completely exhausted and only half-conscious, from his father's hands. Zato noticed everything. His drowsy appearance was mere simulation. Never had his distrust been so intently watchful as at that moment. But he was hungry and his stomach was caving in for lack of nourishment.

The curator was carrying a bunch of fresh bananas.

Without saying a word, he went up to the bars

and handed Zato one of the yellow fruits. He knocked lightly on the iron bar with it and held up the banana.

"Ah, why not eat it?" thought Zato. "Yes, eat it, then we'll be left alone, and then . . ."

He stretched out his arm and, seizing the banana, peeled it with his fingers and teeth. Devouring it with one gulp, he again stretched out his arm with a mute demand that meant "More!" He ate a second, a third.

Suddenly there was no more strength in his arm, it dropped almost before he could raise it, as if it were paralyzed. Even the hand that held Tikki was relaxed and dropped down. Zato's head sank upon his breast. His whole body slumped down, and slid from the wall against which it had been leaning. Zato lay outstretched in the straw, unconscious.

"It's worked," whispered the curator, "and high time!"

He indicated Tikki with his finger.

Tikki had rolled inertly into the straw beside Zato and was hardly moving. He seemed feeble from hunger and half suffocated from Zato's caresses.

Yppa crept up at once, cautiously, anxiously, urged

on by mother love. She picked Tikki up hesitantly, as if she were afraid that Zato might spring up and tear the little thing from her hands.

As nothing happened, she sighed with relief and pressing the baby to her heart, fled.

Chapter Thirteen

A Tame Wolf and a Wild Wolf

HALLO THE TAME WOLF HAD company. Talla, a strong young wolf, had arrived in the zoo, the gift of an important gentleman who could not be refused. They had caught Talla in a pit.

She possessed very little experience as yet, but a rather wild and turbulent nature. When the hunters pulled her out of the hole she had resisted savagely. She came very close to being knifed or shot. But by chance the important gentleman happened to be present. The charming young wolf pleased him. "Take her alive!" he ordered.

So alive she had remained.

To lift her out of the pit they drove her into a narrow box. She gnawed its walls till the splinters flew. They kept her in a small iron cage in the rear-court of the castle. She received an abundance of scraps and the bones from slaughtered lambs and cattle. People would stand before her cage and try to talk amicably with her. Dogs would sniff around and blench back their hair on end along their spines, their lips lifted in a snarl. Talla let nothing disturb or mollify her. She remained consistently filled with rage and bitterness. Had not the bars of her cage been set so close together that she could do no more than force through the tip of her nose, she would gladly have sunk her teeth into every living thing that ventured into her vicinity. She snapped at the huntsmen who brought her food, she snapped at every dog that slunk by. Far back in her narrow cage she sat up on her haunches or lay stretched out, her head between her forepaws, or stood on all four feet, staring out. She saw the geese, chickens, and ducks, the turkeys and peacocks that strutted past, and Talla's eyes sparkled. At night she labored furiously and tirelessly with her teeth at the floor, roof and bars of her cage, scratched with her claws, but everywhere encountered cold iron. Enraged, impatient, and consumed by a fever of desire, she would howl and howl. A hoarse, gruesome, menacing howl.

Oh, to be free! Oh, the glorious, wonderful, free life in the forest! To drink in the cool breath of night! To slink through the thickets, snuffing marvelous scents, scents of young roe, scents of pheasants, of hares slumbering hidden among the lettuce. The spring and catch! The victim's unconscious struggles! Then the intoxicating taste of warm blood, streaming, spurting from the twitching body. Oh, to be free! To slink home to your accustomed or your chosen bed, in the shadiest, deepest thicket as the sun rises and all the four-footed, all the honest feathered citizens of the forest awake from their slumbers. To lie down on dewy leaves and sleep while it grows warmer and warmer! Oh, the free untrammeled existence ... never more. Never more?

All this was in the howling of Talla in the night.

She never did see the forest again. Even the scent of the forest that the wind sometimes wafted temptingly past Talla's longing nostrils was never to be smelled again. But at least it had brought the assurance that the forest was still at hand, the hope of sometime escaping to its green thickets. Now that too was gone.

One day Talla and her iron cage were loaded on a wagon and jolted over the long road to the station.

Talla was to go away. The warmer it became the more the smell of the wolf annoyed the people on the estate. As the important gentleman did not want Talla killed he presented her to the zoological garden, and Talla journeyed to the big city.

She saw nothing of the highroad, nothing of the railroad on which she made her journey. Her iron cage was boarded up so that she was in complete darkness.

Talla could feel only the jolting and rattling of the moving train, which was strange to her. She heard the clattering of the wheels, the snorting and whistling of the locomotive, which terrified her. She breathed coal and oil gas which stupefied her to the point of nausea.

For two nights and two days she lay cowering in a fever of weird and terrible fear. For the first time she was afraid. She suffered racking pains. She felt herself becoming weaker and weaker. For she would neither eat nor drink. Thirst parched her throat and lips. Hunger tore at her stomach. She assumed that profound and endless patience which lulls all wild animals in the presence of death or in captivity.

Finally the moving, rattling and jolting ceased. Her cage was lifted, then dropped with a crash. She thought she would surely die. She trembled for she was rolling along more smoothly now in the midst of strange inexplicable noises. She was on her way from the depot through the streets of the city but she did not know that.

The truck stopped. Once more Talla experienced

that horrible sensation of falling with the box and striking hard against the ground.

Then they removed the boards from the bars. It
was bright daylight. Talla saw the sunshine, saw green
trees and breathed air that seemed to her cool and
refreshing.

She did not move, did not dare to get up. Her state
of drowsy dull drunkenness left her very slowly. But
they did not give her any time. Iron poles prodded her,
driving her out of her narrow prison into the big light
wolves' cage.

Behind her the door rattled shut.

There stood Talla, her tail between her legs, her legs
themselves trembling and swaying, her head sunk low.
Her eyes blinked as if she had been suddenly awakened
after a long, deep slumber. Her parched and painful
nostrils sucked in strangely mingled scents that completely bewildered her.

Hallo, the tame wolf who lived here, approached her
curiously. But Talla's appearance, her peculiar threatening growls, her miserable condition perplexed Hallo. He

stopped a few paces off, wagging his tail a little by way of greeting.

Talla took no notice of him.

After a while she dragged herself, tottering, to the water-trough and drank it dry. Then, ravenously hungry, she seized some food, shook herself, dropped down on the ground, and lying sprawled out on her flank, at once fell into a deep sleep.

When she woke up a day and a night had passed. A new day was dawning.

Talla drank again, and ate the remains of the meal that Hallo had left. He was sitting on his haunches in the open sleeping quarters, watching Talla joyfully. His wagging tail said, "Good morning, I am glad to see you."

Talla did not answer.

He sought to approach her. She lifted her lips in a snarl. "Let me alone!"

Then she looked about. Where was she? What chance was there of escaping? Why was she here? For how long? What would happen to her?

She paced along the semi-circular front of the cage.

To be sure, there was more room to move in. Her limbs, which she had not used for months, were stiff and ached a little. Movement did them good. But there was not a tree, not a bush here, no hiding-place, no opportunity to be alone.

Oh, the joy of being alone! Of being alone and untrammeled! Oh, the undisturbed watching and hunting and seizing! The live prey trying to escape! Talla had forgotten no detail of her former happiness.

She rushed at the bars. Growing wilder she dashed along the semi-circle a dozen times or more, always close to the bars. She bit at the thick iron rods, she scratched at the floor, so unyielding that it did not even show the imprint of her sharp claws. Concrete.

She sat down, panting, her tongue lolling out.

Everything seemed to whirl about her. She wanted time to reflect. Had her misfortune become greater or less? A rage that was really despair blazed up within her. No! No!! No!! was the burden of her short hoarse whining yelps.

Then the young wolf spoke to her. "It's all in vain, my dear, all, all in vain!"

Talla whisked around. "What did you say?"

Hallo approached confidentially. "I've tried it," he continued. "I tormented myself for many days and many nights. You can't escape. Impossible!" He was happy to be able at last to open his heart to someone. "We have to be patient and wait, my dear. That's all. Later perhaps. . . . Perhaps, some opportunity will come . . . sometime . . . perhaps. . . . But who knows," he asked, after a pause, in another tone of voice, "who knows what would happen to us if we did get out? Do you know what it's like out there? No? Well, I know, and I tell you, it's worse than it is in here. . . ."

Talla had got to her feet and walked up to Hallo. He wagged his tail amicably and advanced to meet her. "It's out there that danger really begins. . . ."

Talla pricked up her ears. Her tail began to wag gently. Danger enticed her, lured her. In here there was only torment. But Talla was thinking of the dangers of the forest. And Hallo was thinking of the mysterious incomprehensible dangers of a great city.

"We are too far away," he said, "much too far away! How could we ever find our way home?"

Talla was standing beside him. She snuffed him. For a few seconds only. It was as if she were listening with a marvelously acute sense of hearing.

Hallo stood, all unsuspecting, wagging his tail with joy, and went on speaking.

Then she sprang at him.

The hair bristled along her spine, her lips drew back in an angry snarl, her eyes blazed with fury.

"Coward!" she cried. "Dog! Dog!"

Hallo could not resist the fury of her attack. Startled out of his wits, he fell over and rolled on the floor.

"Where would *you* ever find a home?" he heard Talla in a furious whisper above him. "Where, I say, you traitor, you disgrace to the name of wolf!"

"Let me alone," pleaded Hallo. "Please, let me alone! Oh! Oh!"

He cried piteously, for Talla's teeth were sinking into his shoulder. "What did I do to you?" he whined before she could seize him a second time. "I don't understand you!"

"You don't understand me?" cried Talla threateningly and snapped at him, but a quick movement saved him this time from her murderous teeth. "You don't understand me?"

"No, I don't," whimpered Hallo. "You've hurt me. . . ."

"Do you know the forest, you miserable creature?" Talla raged. She was beside herself. "Do you know what freedom is, you hideous beast? Freedom! Answer me or I'll kill you. Do you know what freedom is?"

"No," howled Hallo, "no! What is freedom?"

Talla leaped at him again, seizing him by the throat. Hallo shrank away and left a tuft of hair in Talla's teeth. She followed him up furiously. "I can smell Him on you, our enemy, the murderous terror! He who tortures us! He with whom there can be no peace because He knows no peace and wants no peace! He who steals the forest from us, who persecutes and destroys us! He whom we hate, whom we despise, whom we fear. Now do you understand me?"

Cautiously, slowly, Hallo crept a little farther away. "No," he groaned.

Again Talla was standing over him. "I smell Him on you. He has made a dog of you, a common dog. . . ."

"He is good!" Hallo sprang up, crying passionately. "He is great and He loves me!"

But Talla sprang at him again with redoubled fury, and drove him into the little sleeping compartment. There she stopped.

"Dog!" she growled. "Don't dare come out! Do you hear?"

"Yes!" Hallo's voice trembled.

"You will die," she growled, "if you dare come anywhere near me. I'll kill you!"

Creeping into the farthest corner of the sleeping compartment, Hallo lay flat on the floor, his nose pointed toward the semi-circle of the cage. Intently he watched his companion.

Another spectator had also watched this scene. Vasta the mouse.

She was a friend of gentle Hallo. From the very first day of his arrival she had been his confidante and comforter. She loved this kind, good-natured, playful companion, who was as gentle with all creatures as a dog. She liked to pass the time with Hallo and he never dreamed of harming her.

He always watched with friendly interest when she drank what was left of the milk, the few drops that sufficed to satisfy her.

She had observed and heard everything, and sat worried, watching her mistreated friend. At last she crept up close to him, and sitting beside his head, which he kept pressed to the floor in fear, she whispered in his ear, "I'll come back and see you later."

Hallo did not venture a reply. He merely blinked understanding.

Vasta ran away. She was so accustomed to the cage that she ran right across the semi-circle. But Talla had

no sooner spied Vasta than she sprang after her, striking out with her forepaw.

Only a desperate leap saved Vasta's life. She felt
Talla's hot breath on her body. She nearly fainted with
sudden fear of death. But she rushed on and escaped.

Outside in safety she had to stop in the middle of
the white gravel path. Her pulse was throbbing even in
her eyes. For a long time she was paralyzed with terror

Chapter Fourteen

Leashed

IT WAS LATE AFTERNOON. THE ELEPHANT was returning from his walk through the zoo. He had been carrying children on his back, seizing them carefully with his trunk, and lifting them on.

At command he would bend his knee and wait patiently until grown-ups scaled his mountainous body. He had carried his keeper on his tusk, lifting him over his head and seating him on his neck.

But the colored saddle-cloth and tower had been unbuckled and he was permitted to leave the cage for a while and wander in the open.

The little white goat that never left his side accompanied him as usual on his tour of the garden and now stood expectantly in the cage beside him.

He received all sorts of gifts from the throngs of people who crowded about the cage. He always gave them all to the little goat, eating only what she spurned.

Close by stood the zoo's two giraffes, silent, patient, slightly sneering.

"You and your goat," whispered Babina, one of the giraffes, to the elephant.

And Zoprinana, the other one, added, "Positively ridiculous."

"Be quiet," trumpeted the elephant. "I like her."

Zoprinana turned her lofty little head. "That's just it. That's just what makes it so ridiculous."

Babina did not trouble to turn her head as she said, "She's no person for you. Such a stupid little thing."

"She's certainly not stupid," the elephant objected.

He stroked the goat's back lovingly. "No, she's not stupid. Talk to her."

But the goat bleated, "I don't want to talk to you, you two long-necked trouble-makers. Besides, why should I worry my head about you? And I don't worry my head about you! Leave us in peace!"

"I am absolutely alone," the elephant said as if by way of deprecatory explanation. "Of course, it's difficult for you to understand that. You are happy, you are together."

"Happy?" sneered Babina.

"My dear, we're dying of boredom," sighed Zoprinana.

"Perishing of homesickness," Babina complained.

"Don't talk about homesickness," the elephant cut her short. "Don't talk about it. Let's not speak of it. I'll go mad if anybody reminds me of it."

He seized sand and small gravel and flung it at the people outside the cage. Everybody laughed.

"You have a splendid time of it," said Babina, "you're permitted to go out, to move. Who knows all the places you go to?"

"Yes," continued Zoprinana, "who knows all that you get to see? With us it's ten paces—twenty all around—and you're done!"

Babina grew passionate. "Consider this tiny cage. Impossible to run, impossible to move as we are accustomed to moving. Our legs are becoming stiff, our joints are hardening. Horrible, the way we are compelled to live here."

"Stunted in mind and body. What is left for us?" cried Zoprinana angrily.

Babina drew herself up. She looked noble, exotic, haughty. But her helpless height, her impotent strength looked somehow silly. Yet she did not sound altogether silly as she said, "What disgusting creatures these must be that come and gape at us every day. What malicious creatures, too, to shut us up this way."

"What sort of mysterious power do they have? You are strong, Pardinos, and yet they captured you. It was not so long ago that you killed one of those hateful creatures. Why don't you kill them all?"

"You could free yourself and all of us," Babina urged, "why don't you do it?"

"There are lions, tigers and panthers here," cried Zoprinana, "we know it although we cannot see them. But we can smell their scent and hear them. You aren't the only one who would be strong enough. . . ."

The elephant smiled. "You two have nothing to fear from me—but lions, tigers and panthers? Would you really like them? Now you are in safety. . . ."

"That is why we hesitated," cried Babina.

"Ho, how brave we are!" laughed the elephant.

"I don't know whether we are exactly brave," replied Zoprinana.

"Bravery is no concern of ours," said Babina, turning her beautiful neck with noble arrogance.

"So there you are," smiled the elephant.

Babina lowered her long neck horizontally in her bitterness. "Do you suppose that those miserable creatures have cooped us up here in order to protect us? Do you really believe that?"

"Bravery or cowardice—it's all one," murmured Zoprinana and drew herself up very erect. "It's all one, I tell you! We would rather have danger and be free. We long to flee when we scent the lion and the leopard in the distance. To flee, our hearts pounding, and conquer our foes by swiftness, then be calm again and watchful. To save ourselves anew every hour, to enjoy our rescued trembling existences tenfold with every hour—that is life, that is what it means to live!"

"Run . . . run . . . run!" Babina was stamping. "That is what it means to live!"

"But to have to stand still here," said Zoprinana quietly, "to have to smell the scent of the lion, to hear him and know that it means nothing—what a terrible fate!"

"Well," said the elephant, rocking back and forth, "we have to compromise. I just as much as the rest of you. . . ."

"You?" Zoprinana regarded him from on high. "You have a good time of it."

"I?" The elephant raised his trunk. "Because they lead me through the garden? What is that little strip of path for limbs like mine? I would like to wander for days and days. With the herd, with my brothers and sisters. I'd like to test my strength on the trees I uprooted, on the tough vines I tore down." He drew a deep gurgling breath. "Do you really suppose that it gives me any pleasure to be led for a brief hour through this horrible garden? Past all those captives pining behind their bars? But I've compromised, otherwise I'd go mad."

"You could fell them with one blow, those crippled creatures with their two legs," breathed the immobile Zoprinana in a tone that was at once provocative and envious.

"I can do nothing!" said the elephant with melancholy decision. "Nothing! They are mightier than we. I don't know why. I don't know by what means. But I do know that resistance is useless."

A blackbird was sitting, a tiny black speck, on the beams that divided one cage from the other. Her little tail seesawed back and forth, her shrewd little eyes

shone like black pearls, her head peeped elegantly now
over one side, now over the other.

"Wrong," she twittered, "wrong! Those two-legged
boobies have no power over me. Not the slightest! They
don't mean a thing. There's not a thing they can do to
me! Not a thing!"

She spread her wings and flew with a twittering cry
to the nearest tree. The giraffes followed her with melancholy eyes.

"Silly creature," muttered the elephant. "Who pays
any attention to her kind?"

At a little distance the gnu was trampling about
madly in his yard. His head was lowered and he was
kicking with his hindlegs, shaking his sparse mane,
bucking in one place so that first his head and shoulders, then his loins and haunches were up in the air.
Presently he would stand tense and still, waiting, as if
plunged in profound thought.

"Alone!" the gnu would grumble. "Alone! And yet not
alone! And yet alone! But the herd is coming! It will
be here any time now! Why do they keep me waiting?

I've waited so long! So long! But there's a lion!" The gnu would crouch, leap up, trampling, lowering his head, beating the earth like a drum with his hindlegs. "One lion? Two lions!"

Then he would stop again, triumphant. "At last I've driven them off! One must defend one's self!"

The gnu gave himself up completely to his daydreams. In this fashion he passed the time.

An axis-deer sauntered by. Small, compact, with very slender legs. A figure of most elegant plumpness. He sauntered to and fro almost solemnly.

When one of the visitors held out a crumb of white bread to him, he would approach the bars reluctantly, as if suspicious or with nicely moderated hauteur, would sniff the crumb, munch it or disdain it according to his humor.

"Why the excitement?" he asked, shaking his head and glancing at the gnu. "Why the excitement? It really doesn't help. Really we get along here quite splendidly."

"Don't we, though?" brayed the gnu. "We wait, we trample a lion or two that attacks us."

"Stop," laughed the axis-deer, "nobody's ever attacked you." He stood with his slender legs spread while his fat cylindrical body quaked with suppressed laughter.

"I agree with you entirely," shouted the gnu, disregarding the remark, "I am quite of your opinion. Everything is splendid here."

A slender gazelle raised its delicate spear-shaped antlers. "One never is attacked here," she chimed in, "and that's a wonderfully comforting feeling."

The axis-deer nodded politely.

At a little distance in the enclosure next to the gazelle lived a roebuck and two does. "What are you discussing?" he asked, coming to the fence.

"We are discussing," said the gazelle, "what a good time we have of it here."

"Yes," he said, "it's very nice."

"And so marvelously secure," she continued, "no attacks. . . ."

"Yes," he agreed heartily, "and no hunting. . . ."

"Hunting?" asked the gazelle. "What is that?"

The roebuck was astonished. "You don't know what

hunting is? Say, you," he called to the axis-deer, "don't you know what hunting is either?"

"No, I don't know either," replied the axis-deer, "is it very bad?"

"Dreadful!" The roebuck grew serious. "When He comes into the forest . . . you don't hear Him, you don't smell Him, you don't see Him. Suddenly he throws his fire-hand at you. It sounds like thunder and leaves you lying in your blood."

"A sensational story," said the gazelle mildly, "but unfortunately not true."

"I don't believe a word you say," declared the axis-deer emphatically.

"Indeed!" The roebuck was offended. "And how did you get here, pray?"

"Not through any fire-hand," replied the gazelle.

"Or any thunderclaps," added the axis-deer.

"And you weren't hunted?"

"I fell into a pit," the gazelle explained, "and He took me out. I remember to this day how I trembled and how frightened I was! But He was friendly to me, and stroked me and gave me something to eat. But the wooden box I was shut in so long was small."

"Yes," declared the axis-deer, "I found the wooden box quite dreadful, too. But otherwise, if what you say is true, why don't they throw their fire-hands around here? Where's the thunder? He would have an easy time of it here."

"How did *you* get into the wooden box then?" asked the roebuck.

"Oh," said the axis-deer, "I had a misfortune. To this day I don't know how it happened. I became entangled in a net in some vegetation I had never seen before. It must have grown up over night, for there it was suddenly in the middle of the jungle, right on the track that I used every day, and had passed over but a few hours previous. A horrible tangling growth of some kind. I got in deeper and deeper. I could never have freed myself, and I was becoming famished. But He freed me."

The roebuck said nothing for a while. "I'm telling you the truth," he said at last. "I've been through hunts many, many times."

"Did you ever lie in your own blood?" the gazelle interrupted.

"No," replied the roebuck, "but my father did. Before my very eyes, and my mother's. I saw Him pick up my dead father and carry him away. Afterwards I often heard His thunder crash, and have seen my cousins and uncles fall as if they had been struck by lightning."

"Incredible!" murmured the gazelle.

"I was a child at the time," the roebuck continued, "quite small. That winter the snow was so deep and I was so weak from hunger that I lay down because I could go no farther. Then He found me."

"And . . ." prompted the gazelle.

"And . . ." inquired the axis-deer.

"And?" brayed the gnu.

"And He saved me," the roebuck concluded.

"If you are not lying to us," said the axis-deer, "I must say, He is more remarkable than I thought."

"At one time bent on murder, at another on kindness," said the gazelle.

"Quite a puzzle," grumbled the gnu.

"Yes, yes," the roebuck ended, "I know more of Him than the rest of you, but I shall never understand Him."

Chapter Fifteen

Separation

HELLA THE HANDSOME LIONESS paced her cage restlessly. Burri and Barri did not know why their mother was so agitated. Barri sprang playfully at her neck and fastened himself to her chin. Hella shook herself slightly as she walked, and Barri fell to the floor, rolling to one side without his mother's taking any notice of him.

Burri was singularly skillful at lying down just in

Hella's path, throwing himself at the last moment right under her feet. She had to stop to avoid stepping on him. This maneuver was always successful. After it the lioness would usually lie down for a moment to surrender herself with a beautiful playful caress to her children's graceful maulings.

But today she avoided Burri's body with a sinuous twist. Or she sprang over him, as gently, as easily, as if her big powerful body weighed nothing at all.

Then, restless, nervous, and worried, she continued her pacing.

She thought: "What shall I do, if it happens again? Suppose they take them from me!" Her heart gave a terrible start. "Burri and Barri, my darlings! Never have I forgotten the others they stole from me, never! But Burri and Barri are such a comfort to me now, a comfort and a joy. Oh what joy! What a tremendous joy!

"But suppose the two children become my sorrow, my despair? How could I ever survive it? Would it not be better if I accustomed myself to do without them now, while they are still with me?"

Troubled, she paced along the outer bars, then along the side to the rear-wall where there was a closed iron door, then along the other side and back to the outer bars. Incessantly, always the same round. Burri and Barri had given up trying to draw their mother into their play.

They paid no further attention to her melancholy mood. She was there, was with them. That was sufficient.

In the middle of the cage they wrestled together, rolling about, kicking their feet, or leaped up, tumbling playfully with their teeth fastened in one another on the floor.

They were charming.

Hella occasionally cast quick glances at them. Quick, loving, delighted glances.

"But I still have them!" the lioness thought with a sudden flood of joy. "I still have them! Perhaps I ought to—but, no, they'll surely let me keep them!"

She lay down on the floor. Instantly Burri and Barri were crawling over her flank, pushing their small velvety paws into her eyes and ears. They tumbled on their backs, puffing their hot panting breath, laughingly, jubilantly, in Hella's face, so that her whiskers quivered.

Hella purred and gurgled with delight.

Before she was aware of it the keeper was standing at the outer bars. "Heh, there, heh!" he shouted, rapping on the iron.

Furiously the lioness started up, sprang at him in a single bound, and stationing herself directly behind the bars, struck out with her claws at this disturber of her peace.

The man stepped back quickly, frightened. "You beast!" he muttered. "She nearly caught me!"

The lioness remained pressed against the bars, growling, never taking her eyes from the man.

He walked past her to see into the cage. Like lightning, she wheeled so that he again found himself confronting her snarling gaping jaws, her enraged and glaring eyes.

He tried to quiet her. "There, there old girl," he said gently, "why so peevish today? What's ailing you? Be nice. We've always been good friends."

He was bothered a little by the visitors who had come running up at the lioness' peculiar short threatening roars.

But his words did not help him at all. The lioness watched every move he made, becoming wilder and more enraged; she growled incessantly.

This was not the hour at which the cubs were taken for a walk. Since early morning the lioness had sensed trouble; she was nervous, upset, and here was the keeper at this unexpected hour.

When he thrust the long iron-shod pole into the cage, Hella struck it down with her paws, fastened her teeth in the cold hard metal and held it fast.

"Stop, be good, old girl," the man tried to mollify her, "stop that!" He was conscious of a guilty feeling. He liked the splendid creature and had possessed her confidence even after her cubs were born and Hella would permit no one near her. She had been docile with him as she lay suckling her young ones which were still blind. For she was grateful to the keeper for boarding up her cage to protect her and her litter from curious eyes. She would purr contentedly when he came to her. And the man had been awed and touched by Hella's motherhood.

Not until he began to entice Burri and Barri away from her day after day, and keep them for hours at a time, did Hella's friendship gradually wane. The memory of her former experience revived in her. She began to recollect more vividly how she had twice lost her cubs, never to see them again, and her trust in this keeper, too, vanished.

She held down the pole with her teeth and paws. But she lost her grip on the smooth pole as the man pulled hard.

The keeper turned to the spectators with an attempt at a smile. "I really don't know what's the matter with her," he declared. "Animals have their moods just like people. Especially the ladies, how they take on! A man always gets the dirty end of the stick. I guess you gentlemen know that, don't you?"

There was some scattered laughter, some of it genuine, some of it mere concurrence. Above it could be heard the furious roaring, snarling and growling of the desperate mother.

"This lady seems to have got out the wrong side of her bed," observed the keeper, "or she's angry at the children."

But he did not feel quite right about it.

He kept trying to open the trapdoor in the partition so that Burri and Barri could run out into the empty adjoining cage. The result was a real contest between him and the lioness.

Then the man lost his temper too. He struck her belly a powerful blow with the pole. She drew back with a howl of pain. He utilized his advantage to open the trapdoor a little way.

But now his difficulties really began.

Burri and Barri who usually obeyed so willingly would not come out. Frightened and admonished by their mother's fury, they were crouching together in the farthest corner of the cage.

The keeper had to pry them out and at the same time ward off the lioness. There was no help for it. He struck her again with the iron-shod pole, this time on the nose.

Her repeated howls of pain had a remarkable effect.

Burri and Barri slunk side by side along the wall and slipped with sudden haste through the door.

When the keeper fetched them from the adjoining cage they were gentle and submissive. But hardly had he taken two steps than they began to scratch and bite with childish rage, so that he was forced to put them down on the grass.

The cubs' sudden action had taken the lioness by surprise. She wanted to hurl herself in front of the hole in the wall, but Burri and Barri were already in the next cage, and the trapdoor suddenly rattled down.

The keeper took no further notice of Hella. She heard him talking to the cubs in the next cage.

She never saw her children again.

The struggle was over and useless. As always.

Hella roared, and it sounded like a vast moan. It sounded as if savage and angry grief were tearing the heart out of her body.

Again and again, this sound of furious sorrow. But no one paid any attention to her. The people ran after the keeper. They crowded around him so that the lioness could no longer see her cubs. Let her roar, complain and moan. No one found it interesting.

Hella sat down on the floor, her forepaws stretched out, her head raised, gazing in the direction in which Burri and Barri had vanished.

She was silent.

Her sides were heaving as she panted feverishly; her tongue hung out.

Hella waited. Hour after hour. Waited till she was nearly exhausted. Waited until her senses were dulled. From time to time, painful longing, or a blaze of anger or false hope would alternate in her brain.

Burri and Barri would come back . . . they would never come back . . . they would play beside her again . . . they would never play beside her again . . . never again. She could not survive it. She could not.

She waited. Resigning herself to a strange, all-powerful, mysterious will, a pitiless fate.

Hella waited. Tamed by the consciousness of utter helplessness, racked by insanely contradictory guesses, and by a dark, remote, inexplicable feeling of guilt that stirred softly somewhere in the depths of her tormented heart.

When the time had passed at which Burri and Barri usually came home, Hella rose and paced about in a circle. Howls of agonized bitter pleading, appealing to something somewhere, appealing to the Unknown. Her agitation increased from minute to minute. Then she stopped pacing, she closed her circle. She sprang against the bars, she assaulted the walls. She howled, she whimpered. She was mad.

Darkness settled down. The blackbird had sung its evening song on the topmost branch of the tree and the highest ridge of the roof, and was still.

The zoo was deserted. It grew dark.

Hella attacked and attacked. Now here, now there. Her throat was bone dry, a hot parched streak ran from her jaws, over the roof of her mouth, to her lips. Her nose too was hot and dry.

"They are gone," said a sad threadlike voice suddenly.

For a moment Hella stood still, listening.

"They are gone," the voice repeated. It was Vasta. "I saw them," said Vasta, "out by the big house where He lives, the lord of the zoo."

Hella stood listening. A shudder passed over her body and her legs trembled.

"They crated them in clean white wood. Yes, both of them together. And a truck took them away. Yes, it's a terrible pity about the dear boys, a terrible pity."

Without a sound the lioness slumped down.

Chapter Sixteen

The Other Side of the Cage

THE MONKEY HOUSE WAS A FLURRY and scurry of life.

During the morning, however, its many inmates lay or sat or crouched rather quietly together. The long-tailed monkeys marched or clambered or sprang about imperturbably, or crouched long and assiduously beside some baboon or lemur giving his fur a thorough examination.

The younger monkeys performed acrobatic tricks

for their private satisfaction and were left for the most part undisturbed.

High up in his corner sat the patient budeng, uneasily scratching his head. As soon as he was left in peace, he grew fearful of what new torments were preparing for him. One thing he was sure of—there would be new torments. And he could never protect himself from them.

A diminutive macaco was running about as if the entire monkey house were his personal property. This was possible only in the early morning.

Now and again, of course, one of the old ones would snatch angrily at the half-grown monkey. But the little macaco would elude him with a burst of indignant scolding which was completely lost in the general silence.

Toward noon the first visitors arrived, men, women and children, young girls and young men. The monkeys crowded closer together. They were critical.

"They're an inquisitive lot out there," muttered a long-tailed monkey.

"But they have power, these creatures, power!" whistled a white-bearded monkey.

"They're stupid," growled a baboon, "painfully stupid!"

This aroused general and enthusiastic agreement. From right and left, above and below, came shouts of concurrence.

"What are they doing here? Every day the same thing, every single day. They stand out there every day."

"But there are different ones every day."

"All the same . . . stupid is stupid!"

"Silly!"

"Repulsive imbeciles!"

A little mandrill joined the discussion with an hysterical outburst. His cheeks, like cracks in fruit, were bright blue up to his angry eyes, his snout was rosy red. "Who says they have power?" he asked caustically. "Who? Can they leap?" he asked. "Can they climb to the top of this cage, eh?"

The others were jubilant.

"Has anybody ever seen them delousing each other?" demanded a macaco.

"Why, they must be alive with vermin," tittered a kahau.

"They haven't even got any fur," shrieked his mate.

"They're all naked, all naked," mocked the kahau.

The tiny macaco pointed to the crowd outside. "You could peel all that off their bodies," he laughed, "and you'd find them as naked and white as their faces—disgusting!"

"Disgusting!" came from the whole circle.

"They stand far below us, these savage, cruel beasts," declared the baboon majestically, "far below us!"

"I roamed around for years with one of them," said a tousled old monkey, coughing. "He covered me with exactly the same clothes he wore himself. What nonsense I had to perform! And how wickedly he beat me!" The monkey coughed.

"Why didn't you bite him?" demanded the mandrill furiously.

"Oh, I bit him often, very often," coughed the monkey, "but . . ."

"But," the kahau completed the sentence, "they are stronger than we."

"Nonsense," cried several, "nonsense!"

"We have the strongest bodies there are," said the baboon. "Just think of Yppa! They'll never be like her, never can be! And they never dream how difficult it is for us accomplished and superior creatures to endure the sight of them. We are the epitome of all that is clever and beautiful, they of all that is unformed, malformed."

"All of us together could soon put an end to them," grunted the mandrill bitterly.

"They are spiteful in their feebleness," mocked the white-beard. "They are afraid of us, mortally afraid, that is why they shut us up."

"Yes, that is why."

"Well said!"

"But they give us tidbits," observed the budeng shyly.

Several of his companions immediately assaulted him, seized his top-knot, pinched and pulled him. He endured their mistreatment for a while, completely submissive and unresisting. Then he fled aloft, crouching, well thrashed, on a little board. Poor fellow, he had never tasted a single one of those tidbits for which he was so grateful.

"In my country," cried the Indian monkey, "in my country we are the lords! We!"

"Do you hear?" they all shouted to the budeng.

"There," cried the Indian monkey, "order holds sway! That naked hairless pack serves us! Us! We can do anything we like! Not one of those base creatures dares disturb us!"

The white-beard caught him by the shoulder. "Then how does it happen that you are here?"

The Indian monkey twitched away indignantly. "A thoroughly stupid question!"

The white-beard pummeled him with both hands. "Simpleton!" he cried furiously. "Braggart! Big mouth!"

The Indian defended himself, snarling and showing his teeth. He rushed all through the cage, glancing over his shoulder to see if he were being pursued. As nothing happened, he sat down beside a long-tailed monkey and busied himself assiduously with its fur.

Meanwhile the white-beard had found a group crouching together and at once sat down among them to denounce the tales of the Indian monkey as lies.

They conversed together mincingly, resolving to take the Indian in hand and pull him to pieces. But another Indian stopped them. "It isn't a lie," he cried passionately, "it's the truth!"

"What's the truth?" the others screamed in his face. "What is?"

The Indian lemur was screeching with the fervor of conviction. "That the world is properly divided there and that we are the victors—that's the truth! That we're worshiped there as is our due! That not one of that naked rabble dares lay a finger on us!"

The white-beard caught him by the shoulder too. "How did the naked rabble come to bring you here then?"

"Those were rabble from another country," answered the Indian in a rage.

As a mocking laugh rose from the circle, he gurgled, almost choking with fury, "They captured us, secretly, maliciously, treacherously!"

"Liar!" snarled the white-beard.

"Babbler! Boaster! Prattler!" sneered the others and attacked him.

But the Indian fought like a devil. The rest retreated.

The people outside stood like a thick living wall. They accompanied the dispute they were witnessing with yells, anxious shouts and bursts of jubilant child-like laughter.

"There's the trouble-maker," said an old man, pointing to the white-beard.

"All monkeys are quarrelsome," observed a young man, knitting his brows fiercely.

"My God!" a plump and rotund woman was heard to say. "My God, just like human beings! We're always fighting and quarreling too."

"*You* are perhaps," growled a smart gentleman in whose eye glinted a monocle.

The rotund woman cast him an offended glance, and appealing to the crowd, was heard to murmur, "I won't stay where there's such a . . . He's probably an officer in civilians or a baron!"

"The idea," the gentleman with the monocle growled after her, "of comparing us to monkeys!"

He awoke no echo. But an elderly spinster observed

to herself, "The sight of monkeys always makes me sad."

"Why?" a shy young man wanted to know.

"Well, they're always sick," explained the spinster.

"Sick," growled a gloomy athlete, "they're dying on their feet!"

The gentleman with the monocle laughed sarcastically. "They're the liveliest corpses I've ever seen!"

"Morituri!" said the shy young man.

But the monocle simply snapped, "Bosh!"

"Their resemblance to human beings is awful," the spinster complained.

"Awful indeed!" agreed the gloomy athlete. Nobody knew in what sense he intended it.

"It is a resemblance that pains and shames," the spinster averred.

"Quite right from your point of view," said the monocle stridently with a smirk.

"They're so helpless," declared the shy one, "so miserable and helpless and that makes their caricature of humans even more terrible. . . ."

"Yes, indeed!" The gentleman with the monocle

made a face as if somebody had insulted him. "Yes, indeed, it is rather a cheeky joke on nature's part."

He wheeled brusquely and departed.

The children uttered a shout of joy, for the little macaco was acting as if he had gone mad.

Somebody had given him a little round pocket mirror.

The tiny monkey saw his reflection in it and was tremendously astonished. He did not know that he was gazing at his own image. He peered over the rim of the mirror to find his new companion, then into the mirror again and was really beside himself. He did not understand it in the least. It was a miracle. He looked at himself, then groped behind the mirror. Again and again, astonished, delighted and perfectly daft.

Laughter from all sides. Children and grown-ups were amused by the droll spectacle. The monkeys became interested and crowded around the macaco. The baboons threw away their bananas, long-tailed monkeys dropped half-oranges, macacos, curl-tails, white-beards and Indian lemurs all cast aside cakes, fruit and sugar and swarmed down to the corner where the tiny creature was sitting.

At the first approach of his larger relatives he had darted aloft like a streak of lightning, and was now crouching high up under the roof, his quick uneasy glances seeking salvation.

Then a wild hunt began.

A baboon reached the little monkey and plunged down after him, swinging from tree to tree, from branch to branch. All the others followed in fierce pursuit.

Once more the tiny creature flew up to the top of the cage as if on wings, his pursuers close behind. Once more he succeeded in reaching the ground. But the others had divided their forces, he was surrounded. There was not a chance to escape.

He raised his thin arms in a gesture of fervent entreaty. The mirror flashed in his tiny hands.

He squeaked, whistled and screamed for mercy. He even ventured to defend himself. He bit, scratched and pummeled. He was heroic.

In vain. His courageous but impotent struggle lasted

scarcely two seconds. They seized him by his four miserable little hands, and it looked as if he would be torn to pieces. They buffeted his head till sparks danced before his eyes.

A baboon wrenched away the mirror and vanished with it.

In a twinkling the others had forgotten the tiny monkey, and the vanquished one, beside himself with despair, slowly climbed down the bars, wailing and scolding.

They all attacked the baboon, but he was not so easy to master. He took up his position in the middle of the cage on the swinging perch where only a few could get at him. There he gazed into the mirror, and though his astonishment did not manifest itself in such wild gesticulations as had the little monkey's, he was so immersed in the mysterious object that he took no notice of five or six powerful monkeys that were sneaking up.

There was an immediate tussle. The baboon sought to flee and he too pressed the little round mirror to his heart. The band rushed madly up and down again. The smaller monkeys dismissed the business, and apparently forgetting all about it, applied themselves to other pleasures or disputes.

Meanwhile the mandrill had confronted the baboon, and succeeded in seizing the mirror from him without a struggle. The mandrill sat still directly in front of the bars. There was no expression at all in his dark eyes or on his colored face. But from his belligerently lifted lip it was plain to see how fascinated he was by his own image, and how intensely he was laboring to fathom the twinkling star in his hand.

Nobody in the cage dared take the prize away from him.

Presently the monkeys had forgotten all about the flat sparkling surface which they had desired so hotly, though now and again one of them in passing cast an envious glance at the mandrill.

Suddenly the mandrill dropped the mirror and clambered away somewhere, perhaps to ponder.

Three or four baboons immediately leaped for it, several long-tailed monkeys joined the chase, again all

wanted to possess the toy. In the course of the ensu-
ing scrimmage the mirror was broken to pieces. Their
greedy hands smashed it to atoms. The miracle was
ended. The mirror was no longer either a mystery or
a puzzle. They seized the little splinters, sniffed them,
tried to see if they were edible, then dropped them, each
with the identical gesture of complete indifference.

One of the many trapdoors that opened into the
winter cage was raised and closed with a loud crash.
The age-old baboon Muffo appeared. His shaggy mane
hung in heavy locks from his shoulders, back and
breast. It enveloped him like the insignia of vast dignity.
His features were grave and thoughtful and there was
something monumental about them as if they had been
cast in bronze. He was the ruler in the monkey house.
He had no intimacies and permitted no insubordina-
tion. If his favor was won for an indefinite time, no one
ever knew why. If it was lost again, with a sudden fall
from grace, no one ever knew why. No one ventured to
resist him, no one permitted himself any familiarities.

Slowly, with a reserve betokening great wisdom, he

wandered through the cage, and to all the monkeys it seemed as if he were bringing them a weighty decision.

It grew more quiet. All feared his wisdom, his strength and his terrible humors.

Muffo found the little splinters of broken mirror and picked one up. Examining it as one examines anything with which he has long been familiar, he tossed it away with a gesture expressive of much superior disdain.

Then he seated himself on the stone ledge in the front of the cage, leaning against the bars, so that the people outside could see nothing but his broad and hairy back.

Turning his face to his people, he began to speak. "Another fraud with which to hoax us—just an attempt to divert our lively intelligence with a silly toy." He held a splinter of the mirror between his fingertips and tossed it indifferently on the sand. "The naked ones are afraid of us!" he cried, rumbling sullenly.

"They will have to worship us!" cried the Indian ecstatically.

"Silence!" snarled Muffo harshly.

The Indian was terrified.

After another pause Muffo spoke again. "The end is coming soon in spite of the naked ones and all their cleverness." He drew a deep breath. "The day will come!"

All the monkeys were ravished.

Chapter Seventeen

Free

"I WAS HERE ONCE YEARS AND YEARS AGO. Father and mother brought me on a Sunday."

The young man was talking to his companion as they passed between the row of parrot-cages to the lawns with their beds of blooming flowers. The girl simply nodded and said nothing. When they reached the monument to the dead chimpanzee the young man caught her arm. "Say, that's new!" he exclaimed.

The girl laughed. "No, I've seen that ape there for ages."

"Yes, *you've* seen it," said the young man, "but I . . ."

"Well, why haven't you?" she asked.

"I told you I was only here once."

"Only once?" She was astonished.

"Yes," he repeated, "only once. As a little boy. Never again."

"Comical," she murmured.

He was a pallid fellow, barely thirty, with a broad-boned face in which boyishness, brutality and dreaminess combined to produce a remarkable expression. Sometimes his brown eyes were tender and mild and longing. Sometimes they burned with a gathering rebellion and at such times they would become quite small for a moment, with something in them of crafty patience. When he took off his cap one could see that his close-cropped black hair grew low on a forehead that was not too lofty. His clothes were poor, but neat, even a bit modish. A factory worker on his Sunday off.

She wore no hat, and her bobbed, very much waved, very luxuriant blonde hair fluttered about a small, but pretty face whose rouged lips were like a silent shriek.

Elsewhere she had no need of rouge. She had a short, charming snub-nose, and merry gray eyes. She wore a silk dress of Scotch plaid and a dark blue coat that just reached to her knees. This outfit revealed, while seeming to conceal, disclosing the sturdy body of a twenty-year-old girl, with its firmly modeled slender legs and small joints. There was something indolent, something wayward that was quite without shyness—in her walk, in her gestures, even in her face. In her joyous manner was the assurance of a pretty young girl who is conscious of her power. But there was also a trace of kindliness, of strong maternal instinct.

He read the inscription on the monument: "To Peter the Chimpanzee." Then the date. "So they've erected a monument to the poor fellow," he said. "But what did he die of? The inscription doesn't say."

"Oh, you know, Max," said the girl. "The monkeys in the zoo all die of consumption."

"Or from imprisonment," he added bitterly, "which comes to the same thing." He had not released her arm. "Come, Mieze," he growled, dragging her along. "A monument to a monkey! I'd like to know what sense there is in that. They ought to erect a monument to commemorate the crimes committed against monkeys. That would be smarter."

Mieze gave him a little smile. "What's the use of getting excited, Max?"

A soft dreamy expression came into his eyes. "You said 'comical' before. Why?" He was answering her previous exclamation. "It wasn't comical at all. I was really here just once. You know how it is with poor people. I was ten or twelve years old at the time. My parents happened to have a little money and that's probably why they were good to one another and also to me. Well, we came here together."

"But Max," Mieze quieted him, pressing the hand that held her upper arm against her body. "I didn't mean anything by it, Max."

He paid no attention. "Probably I would never have come here otherwise. My mother took sick a few weeks later and by autumn she was dead. I had to go to school shortly after and my father..." He was silent for a while and a little fire flickered in his half-closed eyes. "Well," he added, "when you begin to work, you don't think about such things." His sweeping gesture included the whole park.

They were approaching the cages, moving in the stream of visitors, when Max stopped. "Ah," he said softly, "ah, the trees, the free green leaves, and the free sky above. Ah, it does you good, it's fine, that's what people need. . . ."

He gazed up at the tree tops, at the blue sky and the white and golden clouds floating overhead; his face was quite innocent and boyish. "Look, the flowers, Mieze," he whispered close to her ear, "look, the flowers in the beds. I wish that stupid monument hadn't been there."

"You're a monkey yourself," she said.

"No," he shook his head, "you can't imagine what it's like." He interrupted himself. "Thank God, you have no idea. But when you haven't seen all this for two years, when you've all but forgotten it, how beautiful the world is!"

"So it's all the flowers and trees," laughed Mieze,

"and I'm nobody. Ouch!" she cried. He had dug his finger into her arm. "Stop, Max! Are you crazy?"

He stopped. But he really was quite crazy.

Suddenly he stopped short, completely sobered, an entirely different person. His cheeks had gone pale and his manner was surly as he dragged Mieze quickly down a side path.

"What is it?" she asked frightened. He did not answer. "What is it?" she asked again, more agitated. For a long time he said nothing. She did not dare utter another word, but simply saw out of the corner of her eye how his eyes narrowed, became crafty and filled with suffering. When he had collected himself again, when his chalk-white face had resumed its accustomed pallor, he said in an offhand tone, "It was somebody I don't want to meet, one of them from in there . . . you know. . . ."

She understood and said nothing.

"He was let out three weeks before me, the dirty dog," he said after a pause.

"What do you care?" asked Mieze loftily.

"Nothing at all! But for all that, I don't want to meet him, the cheap safe-cracker!" He was angry. "That fellow said that I'd never find a job again! Why? Because of what happened to me? Can I help that? Tell me, am I a criminal because of that?"

"You did it in self-defense," said Mieze gravely.

"Exactly," cried Max in a rage, "exactly. If I hadn't had my knife, Tony would have made a cripple of me or killed me. He's a wild man. I'm sorry that it had to be that way, but better him than me!"

Mieze pressed his hand. "You were in there nearly two years," she said sadly.

"There, you see!" Max was tremendously angry. "And I don't want to meet anybody from in there out here! Nobody! Those scoundrels! They'd like to pull you in with them all right! That dog I just avoided was always trying to get me to work with him. Huh, he calls that *work*!"

Mieze soothed him. "Be quiet, my love, don't think about it! Be happy that it's over!"

"I *am* happy," he shouted almost hilariously.

"We're together again," laughed Mieze.

Max said nothing, looked at her and laughed happily. They walked along and came to the enclosures of the giraffes and the elephant.

"I've never seen such creatures since I was a little boy," he said.

"It always seems to me as if I were seeing fairy tales come true," said Mieze. "They can't be real!"

"What are they then?" asked Max. "They're just as real as you or me."

They stood for a while watching the animals in silence, then went on.

"Speaking of fairy tales," he said, "my spending a whole day here with my parents, which was real enough, seems like a fairy tale to me now. I try to recall my mother or my father—I can't do it! I can't see either one of them. I can't remember anything at all, not a thing! And yet it was a day just like this."

"Look, over there!" cried Mieze. "The monkey house!" She hurried over and he followed her. Then they stood for a long time wedged in among the crowd, watching the antics of the long-tailed monkeys, baboons and lemurs.

Mieze laughed aloud several times at the gymnastics, the leaping, the pursuits, the stratagems, the mistreatment and the bravery of the little monkeys, at their squeakings, barkings and vociferous growls.

Max did not move a muscle of his face.

"It's the same wherever you go," he said when they left. "The strong beat the weak and take the food out of their mouths!" There was a gentle irony in his tone as he said, "You could almost believe it's a welfare institution."

Mieze caught up his irony and embroidered it. "But it's just another monkey house!"

They both had a feeling of satisfaction as if they had told the world something. Max and Mieze gazed into one another's eyes. Their hands clasped and they were perfectly happy. Mieze saw the people running to the lion house. "Look, look, something's happening there." She began to run too. Max followed her. He was delighted at the graceful way in which she ran ahead of him, at the ingenuousness of her movements, revealing the little schoolgirl that Mieze had been not very long ago. There was a kind of hesitancy in his gait; his body, his limbs seemed to be not yet wholly free, seemed to be impeded still by fear and prison discipline. Mieze stopped and turned to him: "Hurry up! Quick, quick!"

They arrived just as Barri and Burri were being taken away from their mother. Hella's futile resistance was over. Driven on by the keeper, the two little lions were trotting awkwardly along accompanied by a crowd of excited people. Max and Mieze let the procession pass. Barri and Burri stumbled, rolled into balls and tried to go back. They struggled and while the people laughed, the keeper kept them moving in the direction he wanted. Max was in a cheerful, if slightly cynical humor. He pointed to the cubs, saying jestingly, "Proletarian childhood!"

"But don't they say," Mieze rejoined, "that the lion is the king of beasts."

"What do you mean, king?" said Max with a smile. "He's a prolo here!"

"Maybe," said Mieze, "but they don't know much about such things."

"Very likely," Max agreed. "Just look at them. They don't know anything, of course not. But are they happy? Not so that you could notice it. Happy children have a different look. And some day they're going to run wild. Against authority, against injustice! One king is as good as another, and it won't be any joke when the wild beast awakes in the workingman!" He talked with the force of a speaker addressing a meeting.

Hella roared in her cage. A deep moan, as if something were tearing her breast.

Mieze turned to look at her, and Max followed Mieze. They were the only people standing before the cage. Hella's features were distorted with pain, while from her throat broke wild moans. Her wide open jaws revealed her dangerous fangs as she uttered the terrifying elemental sounds of despair.

In the neighboring cages, to the right and left, then farther away, the other beasts of prey took up Hella's maternal wail. The old circus-lion thundered so that the air seemed to quiver. Mibbel rumbled from a heavy heart. The tiger howled terrifyingly, voraciously, imperiously. From the panther came sharp, crying, howling sounds.

Mieze, who felt a little strained and a little bored, tugged at Max's arm. "Let's go."

Unhearing, he did not even move. He was quite numbed. His face had become chalk-white again and the color had faded even from his lips. His chin quivered. He stood listening to the untamable languages of those voices of revolt. He was stirred by the impotence with which this elemental outbreak died away, unheeded and unheard.

"Jail," he whispered, "jail. When one of them begins shouting, they all begin shouting. And not one of the keepers pays the least attention to it."

He was whispering in the midst of the uproar about him, and became more and more aroused. "Nobody hears their ravings, not one of the righteous judges who imprisons human beings behind bars!"

Mieze was silent.

"Do they know what they're doing?" cried Max passionately. "Do they ever dream how many souls they murder, how much goodness they destroy? You can't punish and reform at the same time! They just don't go together!"

He turned to Mieze, apparently calm and rational. But she could see how upset he was. "I tell you, some of those fine gentlemen ought to sit once behind the bars. Just once. Cut off from the world, deviled, looked down upon, helpless and defenseless. They ought to try it, only for a month or two, and sit in there where a man ceases to be a man. Maybe they'd understand then that they and their jails breed more evil than all the criminals in creation! Maybe they'd understand. . . ."

"Lord," Mieze interrupted, "how worked up you are! Come, let's go! It would have been better if we hadn't come here at all."

"Yes, let's go," replied Max a little more calmly. "You're right. I'll simply be upset here. But it's a good thing that we came. A very good thing! These creatures," he included all the cages in a sweeping gesture, "these creatures here are my companions in suffering, so to speak. Indeed they are! I have respect and I have pity for them. For after all," his voice sank to a whisper, "after all I defended myself against a bully, but they never did anything, nothing at all. . . ."

He stopped. "Yes, it's a good thing that we came here," he said. "This is a place where a poor devil can see the injustice and the cruelty of the world plainly enough. You can see how people stroll past suffering, tortured creatures and don't care any more for them than that. Aren't even amused by them. And—do you know, Mieze, that kind of comforts me."

Mieze clasped his arm and they hurried away.

Hella's moans and Brosso's dull roaring sounded behind them.

Max turned. "Yes, go on roaring. You're right!" And he added with the ghost of a smile, "But what good does it do to be in the right, what good does roaring do, when nobody pays any attention to it?"

Chapter Eighteen

"He Wants No More of It"

ZATO THE ORANGUTAN AWOKE from his long stupor.

When Yppa observed that her mate was beginning to show signs of life she held Tikki tight in her arms and fled into the farthest corner of the cage. For several hours she had watched for Zato's revival. She was afraid he would be violent. Again and again she had been terrified by the thought that Zato would tear his little son from her arms, would attack her in a fit of rage and abuse her.

Now Zato had moved. Yppa fled as far away as she could get and sat cowering in her corner, peering through half-closed blinking eyes, shyly, at the body stretched out on the floor. With her arms and hands she hid Tikki as well as she could.

"Why haven't they taken Zato away?" she wondered. "Why haven't they put back the wall that separated us when Tikki was born?"

Zato groaned softly. After a while his arms groped slowly and uncertainly in the air.

Then he sat up.

He stared straight ahead of him. Everything seemed to swim before his eyes—those eyes that were like those of a drunkard or a man dying for sleep.

Hour after hour he stared thus.

When the keeper came and tossed him fruit he did not stir. He remained motionless when the curator appeared and talked to him through the bars.

"Well, my boy," said the curator in a friendly voice, "sleep it off? Have a good rest?"

Zato sat as if he had heard and seen nothing.

"You must understand that it was necessary, my friend," continued the curator, "so that your little son would not starve. You were so obstinate, there was nothing else to do. Now treat your family nicely and we'll do the same to you." The curator turned to the keeper. "Let's go. He'll pick up overnight. Even a human head would ache a little after coming out of that kind of veronal debauch."

But Yppa trembled at the thought of the night. She felt dreadfully certain that Zato was sitting there so silent and indifferent because he was controlling himself, pretending. Terrified, she was convinced that Zato was only waiting for darkness to leave her alone with him. Then he would attack her and the child, would choke her, and kill poor Tikki. She did not dare move, but she was a little comforted by the fact that Tikki was sleeping on her breast and so made no noise that might excite Zato.

From the time that darkness settled down until morning broke, she continued in a state of panic that robbed her of her breath, then became a more and more relaxed anxiety.

Zato had not once changed his position. He had not made a sound.

When the first feeble light permitted her to distinguish objects Yppa glanced at her mate. He was sitting in the same place: he had not moved. As it grew lighter, just before sunrise, Yppa gathered courage to turn her head cautiously and stare curiously at Zato. His head had sunk down upon his breast. After the fashion of unhappy orangs, he had laid his face in both hands. He seemed to be asleep. But Yppa knew that Zato was awake.

She was terribly tired. In her state of total exhaustion she no longer had the strength to be worried. She no longer cared what happened to her or to Tikki.

Thus the morning passed and half of the afternoon.

Tikki became lively and Yppa let him do as he liked. When she observed that the little thing avoided his father she let him run free.

The second night passed without any change. Zato

seemed to sink deeper and deeper into himself. He did not take the slightest notice of Yppa or of Tikki. The fruit that was tossed him lay dried up or rotting. He had not even glanced at it.

In time his condition began to worry the curator. He stood before the bars, talking kindly to the orangu-tan. But after all they were utter strangers. Zato did not hear the man, or if he heard, did not understand him. He did not give him a thought.

The curator spread rare and tempting fruits before the orang. Zato left them untouched.

Once Yppa approached Zato, timidly, tenderly. Timidly she held out Tikki to him, like one ready for sacrifice.

Zato did not move.

"Tikki is here," she whispered, "right beside you, Tikki whom you love so much."

In vain. The words fell upon deaf ears.

The little one resisted violently, trying to avoid his father and clinging to his mother with every sign of terror.

Hours later Yppa again went to Zato, and sitting

down at his side put her arm around his shoulder. She sat perfectly still beside him. But Zato's rigidity did not relax for a moment. Yppa might just as well have embraced a block of wood. She was frightened. She picked up the fruit, picked it up piece by piece from the floor and held it before Zato's mouth. He did not refuse, he did not resist. He was inaccessible, hard and strange, as lifeless as the walls. Yppa ate a little to arouse his appetite. He did not even see her.

That night she slept beside him, pressing her body softly against his, stroking, caressing him. But there was not the slightest response, not the slightest sign that he was aware of her. Her gentle appeals remained unanswered. She could embrace only one side of his body, nestling close to his ribs and thigh. He did not change his position, sitting with his hands over his face, his head sunk low upon his breast.

Next day a scene took place that shocked Yppa. It shocked the curator too. He was standing outside the cage with Dr. Wollet. He had brought choice fruit and was talking again very gently.

Suddenly Zato got up. His limbs stirred very slowly, almost solemnly. His eyes were fastened on the curator. His big dark eyes had seemed sad even before. But what an expression was in them now! An expression of the most intense pain, the patience of martyrdom, an expression of farewell that was already directed from the hither side of life, from the beyond. It shocked the two men who saw it.

They were silent. Dr. Wollet struggled to keep back the tears that were smarting in his eyes.

Zato accepted a banana and peeled it. Slowly. Solemnly.

"Thank God," said the curator very softly, "he's going to eat at last."

With a voice choking with emotion Dr. Wollet replied, "He will not eat again."

Zato carried the banana to his mouth. Then he broke and mashed it and dropped it on the floor. He took some grapes, and put them to his lips as if he were going to kiss them. Then he clenched his fist and squeezed the grapes so that the juice oozed between his fingers.

Always that expression of ultimate pain and knowledge.

A shudder passed over Zato's gigantic body.

Dr. Wollet turned away, he could not bear it. "He
will never eat again!" he repeated in a low voice.

"Nonsense!" declared the curator. "Even a human
being has to eat no matter how bad he feels. Certainly
an animal must."

"But, but," cried Dr. Wollet, "how can you say that?
Think of the dogs that won't eat another mouthful after
their masters die, but follow them to the grave."

"Stop," the curator interrupted. "I know your hobby!
The animal belongs to a higher order than man. But in
spite of your love of animals, you'll never make me . . ."

"Not higher in any sense!" Dr. Wollet replied. "But
not lower either. Not much lower! The lower charac-
teristics in us and in them just about balance. As for
the human mind, that sublime and godlike mind—there
may be some significance in the fact that animals do
not lie, are honest and are quite without a sense of guilt."

The curator raised his hand to allay and to dismiss.

"Your hobby is carrying you to absurdity at a gallop!"

"Don't laugh!" Dr. Wollet became emphatic. "How can you look at that and laugh?" He motioned with his head toward the cage.

"I'm not laughing," the curator protested. "I perceived before you did that this is a serious case."

Zato sat hunched over, hiding his head in his hands.

"So savage a determination to end matters," continued Dr. Wollet pointedly, "so grim and persistent a renunciation of life, is found but seldom among humans. And when it is found, it is only among exceptionally elementary natures!"

"As if it were an everyday occurrence among animals," cried the curator.

"This whole garden," said Dr. Wollet angrily, "this whole garden is filled with elementary tragic figures! The whole world is filled with the tragedies of dumb creatures in which the human always gets the better of the beast!"

The curator's shrugging shoulders betrayed his impatience.

Dr. Wollet said nothing for a few moments. Then he spoke quietly, in a calmer tone, only the frequent catches in his voice betraying how disturbed he was.

"This orang," he said, "who was drugged and captured, who was dragged from his jungle into this terrible prison of stone and iron, this orang found one little remnant of joy, perhaps of happiness. In any case he found some faint consolation for all he had lost in his mate—and in his child."

"He would have starved it to death," the curator interrupted.

"Perhaps . . . who knows? But he was drugged again, and that little shred of courage, that tiny trust that let him live was snapped. It dissipated like a little drop of water that you brush away unawares with your sleeve."

"It was done in the interest of the baby, in the interest of the mother," said the curator nervously. "And it was in his own interest, too, that we gave him veronal."

"Possibly. But he doesn't understand your expedients, and he doesn't understand veronal. He doesn't trouble himself about what you call his best interests.

He has had enough of the mysterious craft that makes his life wretched. He wants no more of it."

Dr. Wollet was close to the truth. Zato wanted no more of it.

Neither Yppa's tenderness and imploring appeals, or Tikki who hopped about comically, existed for him. Zato took no nourishment and seldom stirred from his place. One day he lay stretched out on the floor, cold. A peaceful sleeper.

Yppa was alone with her child.

Chapter Nineteen

The Miniature Reporter

VASTA THE MOUSE CARRIED THE melancholy news to every cage in the zoo.

When she came to Hella she found Mibbel the lion with her. Hella was pacing about nervously in a circle, with Mibbel trotting leisurely after her. He would tease Hella by nestling his light short-maned head against her shoulder, her flanks, her chin, whatever he could reach. But whenever he touched

Hella she drew back angrily and seemed on the verge of an outburst. Mibbel did not notice or did not want to notice anything. He continued to purr contentedly and to chat while purring.

Vasta sat in her crack in the wall, astonished at Mibbel's urbanity, her clever inquisitive eyes fixed on him.

"Really, Hella," Mibbel was purring, "you should hear Brosso some time. You have no idea of all that he's been through. I can't even begin to imagine it all." He rubbed his head against her shoulder. She bounded lightly away to avoid his caress, changing the direction of her walk. "All Brosso's experiences are so exciting," he purred. "It was wonderful to be together with him, although I'm very happy to be allowed to stay with you again." He pushed his head affectionately against her flank. Hella drew back and continued pacing. Mibbel followed her. "A splendid old boy, this Brosso," he purred, "you ought to see and hear him. Yet he's friendly and gentle. Of course, he's lost a great deal of his strength. A great deal. What a powerful fellow he must have been! Even today he is strong enough to . . ."

Hella faced about and began to trot. Three or four steps in one direction, three or four in the other, with Mibbel close beside her. "Well, perhaps Brosso will come to stay with us, too," he said. "That would be wonderful! What splendid entertainment! None of us has ever been through the things he's experienced."

Hella threw herself on the floor. "I think," she muttered, "I think I've been through enough, more than I care for!" She sighed deeply.

Mibbel was dancing around her. "Oh, you mean the cubs," he said lightly and not very sympathetically. "The cubs! I understand what you mean. But don't be sad. There's no sense to it and it doesn't help at all."

"You never knew them," growled the lioness.

"No," he said hastily, "no, I didn't know them. I only saw them a couple of times as they passed by. Nice boys, very nice. . . ."

A piteous howl was her answer. "Nice? They were charming, they were fascinating, and so clever! Nice! It's easy to see that you never knew them."

"Well, it's not my fault; I would have liked to see

them. I wanted to be together with you and them," Mibbel protested.

"Not your fault?" repeated Hella. "Who knows?"

"Forget the little fellows," urged Mibbel, "there's nothing else to do. We must all of us learn to forget if we want to live."

"Forget?" snarled Hella angrily.

Zealously he tried to pacify her. "You managed to forget the cubs you had before."

Hella started up. "You heartless creature! Do you really believe that?"

Mibbel fled to the bars in one terrified bound.

Hella was furious. "I always remember all of my children! You, you heartless wretch, think I don't because I say nothing. But they are all of them in my heart, all of them, always, forever. . . ."

"Why do you grieve?" wailed Mibbel. "They're all right. They're gone, of course, but they're all right. I feel positively certain of it!"

"Ugh!" Hella's contemptuous grunt was accompanied by a disdainful toss of her head. Then she went to the back of the cage and lay down against the wall.

Vasta took advantage of the silence that followed to whisper her news to the lioness. Hella listened attentively, pitying Zato.

"Think of Yppa," said the mouse. "Now she is all alone."

"She has her child," replied Hella.

"But she has lost her mate," warned the mouse. "Remember that when you become angry at Mibbel. He's alive, he's well and strong, he is handsome and he loves you." With that she slipped away. She was in haste.

Hella remained for a long time lost in thought. But when Mibbel slunk up to her, meekly and cautiously, he perceived from the beating of the tassel on her tail, and from her manner, that she was in a friendlier mood.

"Are you still angry at me?" he asked. She looked at him as he snuggled against her side. "I am stupid," he purred. "You are right, that business about the children was hateful. . . ."

Hella laid her beautiful head between her forepaws. "Oh, my good friend," she said softly, "it is not a question of forgetting. You can't forget even if your memory is as short as ours seems to be. But we must learn gentleness and patience if we want to live."

Vasta carried the news to the bears' cage.

She often visited the big brown clumsy fellows. They were good-natured and playful, always fond of their joke, and they never grudged the mouse a bite from their abundance. Vasta was on friendly terms with the bears.

This time she was the witness of an exciting scene.

Krapus, the tall strong bear, was sitting on his haunches, craftily watching Karl, the keeper, who was cleaning out the cage.

Driven to the back of the cage by Karl, the other bears one by one relinquished their places with angry growls and suddenly bared teeth.

Karl was cross with them. He poked his broom at their noses, between their eyes, in their flanks. If he came too near the bears did not wait for the blow. Tripps, the thin little bear, shambled nimbly out of the way. Papina, who would presently have cubs, toddled out of reach. Halpa, the girl bear, was frightened and betook herself to safety.

All of them knew keeper Karl's humors. His many tokens of friendliness no longer meant anything to the bears. They were vengeful with all the strength of their good natures, and dangerously cunning in their thirst for vengeance. Karl miscalculated this. He was in one of his surly morning moods. He swaggered around like a bully, taking out his temper on the bears.

Only Krapus remained steadfastly and stubbornly in his place. He sat up on his haunches, as if waiting for a signal to begin the battle, or for the right moment to attack. He would not be dislodged by keeper Karl. But Karl appeared to have little desire to challenge Krapus. He was in a bad humor, he knew very well why the bears were aroused. But that threatening glimpse of Krapus' plump power was so fatefully imposing as to penetrate even Karl's surliness. He wanted to avoid the furious beast and, bridling his own temper, turned to leave the bears' cage.

At that instant Krapus sprang forward and struck

at Karl with the full force of his fury. The three other bears watched with intense interest. Obviously the attack had been planned, obviously they all knew of it and were merely waiting to pounce on the keeper the moment he fell to the ground.

Karl would have gone down without a word, but with a fractured skull, if Krapus' furious paw had ever reached him. But the terrible blow fell short and whisked through the air as Krapus lost his balance and fell.

Then Karl's rage became a frenzy without let or hindrance, delivering him from that oppressive feeling which had weighed on his heart all morning.

Before Krapus could stumble to his feet, Karl attacked him with the broom, striking him on the nose with the iron handle, three, four, five times, catching him always on the same sensitive spot.

"You beast, you!" cried Karl in a husky voice. "You dirty beast!"

His courage gone, Krapus fled. Then, racked with pain, he tried desperately to defend himself. He stood up, thirsting for vengeance, but another terrible blow on his nose brought him low.

Karl did not stop beating him until his rage had cooled, and Krapus, completely vanquished, had crept into a corner, hiding his nose between his paws.

"You wait, you dirty rascal!" muttered Karl before leaving the cage. "I'll show you yet!"

In their fear the other bears pretended to be innocent and peaceable, but Karl did not believe them.

"You damned rascals!" he shouted. With that he left them.

Vasta had watched, greatly disturbed.

Papina, the bear who was going to have cubs, sidled over. "Tell me, little friend," she said, "you are free, you are more fortunate than we, tell me, is there no help for us?"

Vasta considered, and for answer told them what had happened in the orangutans' cage.

"Oh," cried Halpa, "there is no help for us captives. He is too strong and He is cruel. He knows no mercy!"

But Vasta had flitted away.

She ran to the regal tiger. She loved his majestic beauty, his proud strength. She respected his noble reserve, the disdainful hauteur that made him a solitary. She admired the impenetrable, unfathomable quality of his nature. She would feel terribly unstrung when with condescending kindness he spoke to her. At such times she was aware of the enormous gulf dividing him from her.

Opomo, the splendid young regal tiger, lay quietly in the middle of his cage. His forepaws stretched out, his head thrown back, he was gazing through the bars at the green and blooming garden. He was no longer conscious of the iron bars, they seemed to have become a part of the garden, black streaks striping the bright green of the trees and grass. They could not be removed, they belonged inseparably to his world.

He had never known any other. Some three years before he had entered this cage. He had left his mother very early. The things she told him when he lay against her breast as a little cub he no longer remembered. He remembered only the affectionate games they had played together. His mother too had been born behind the bars, and behind the bars she had grown up. Where she was at present he had no idea, and indeed, thought of it very seldom and never for more than a moment or so.

Ever since leaving his mother he had been almost always alone. Once he had had a mate. For a short time he admired and loved her passionately. One night she disappeared mysteriously from his side and for a brief period he mourned her.

For a long time the cage with its strong iron bars, the walls that enclosed him, had seemed to him simply a part of an unalterable fate to which he had resigned himself. When he was quite young he used to hurl himself furiously, to the point of exhaustion, against the bars and the walls. Now that was all passed. He had become dull, he thought of nothing. He stared into space and saw nothing. The garden outside seemed simply a bright green dissolving effect. Like insubstantial shadows human beings sauntered past his cage.

Vasta sat still in her hiding-place, worshiping

Opomo. The tiger's careless, soft, powerful grace possessed a fascination for Vasta. She could never free herself from the thrall of his beauty. Each time she resolved to visit the tiger she was torn between fear and temptation. Once she was safely in her hiding-place in his cage it required an effort to compose herself.

Opomo had snuffed her scent. He turned his head in her direction, otherwise remaining motionless. But he began to purr very softly.

A brief pause—then suddenly he questioned her. "What news, little one?"

"The great father ape, Zato, is dead," Vasta instantly answered.

The tiger, trembling, bounded up—and then at once lay down again. "Tell me about it!" he commanded.

Overwhelmed with terror, Vasta had fled. The tiger's command fetched her back. Stammering and trembling, she made her report. She knew practically the whole story. She even knew of the orangutan's homesickness.

As she reached this part of her story the tiger got up. With that springy tread in which his whole body was involved the tiger paced around the cage, betraying increasing agitation.

"Homesickness," he groaned, "homesickness! Can that longing, that blind aimless longing that tears me to pieces, that drives me almost insane, can that be home-sickness?" He stood still, with lowered head, while from the bottom of his heart came a roaring moan—"Home-sickness!"

"Night and day it torments me! Before the sun rises, and in the last hour of twilight. When I lie sleeping, I dream, I dream! Wonderful dreams! I think that I am yearning for my dreams!

"Homesickness!" He began to rave. "There must be something somewhere, some land, I don't know where! Trees, tall grasses! There must be! There must! That's what I see in my dreams! Oh, the slinking along, the watching, the spring at something alive that crumples under your claws. The warm blood that spurts out—in your mouth, in your eyes!" He raved on. "Must I spend my whole life here, in this miserable, stinking, horrible prison . . . my whole life! Must I never experience the things I experience in my sleep, in my dreams—such pale unreal things! A prisoner! A prisoner! Now I know what I am—a prisoner!"

Vasta had slipped away. In the distance she heard the tiger whom she loved so dearly. Her tiny little body was quaking with nervousness. She felt herself in the grip of the violent storm which her news had unchained. That is why she hurried to the two black panthers whom she seldom visited. She was afraid of them. But she felt that she must bring them the news, she wanted to see how they would receive it.

They scented and spied her out at once.

"She's sitting there again!" purred Solb, the elder of the pair, puffing his hot breath at her.

"Yes, I saw her!" growled Fasso, the smaller, snarling at her.

Only the wall protected Vasta, and her knowledge that in the crack of the wall she was safe. The two panthers drummed, scratched, beat against the wood in their effort to catch the little mouse. Had they ever reached Vasta she would have lain there in less than a second, a tiny, unrecognizable scrap of bloody flesh. The panthers' sharp claws beating against the smooth-painted wall sounded like the fall of hail.

Vasta contentedly polished her pointed nose, but she did so partly to quiet her nerves which began to jump at the sight of the panthers.

Presently Solb gave up the attack and Fasso immediately followed his example.

They began to run about their narrow cage. They were dancing, if one observed them closely, with noiseless, marvelously light steps and sinuous movements of their bodies. It looked as if they really had no bones, as if their limbs were made of silk floss, of black velvet, of firm but elastic rubber. They ran one after the other, executed a figure, and came together again. They executed many changing figures while their black and mobile bodies responded to a silent music full of deep harmonies, full of untamable wildness which could never be softened and of dangerous surging primal power, which continually thrilled them, to whose perpetual ecstasy they must surrender themselves, and which was perpetually renewed in their surrender. It was a dance of impatience, a dance of despair. It was the dance of the captives.

In a piping voice Vasta imparted her news.

The panthers sprang into the air, weaving back upon themselves, weaving one about the other. They would not let Vasta go on.

"What do we care about the orang?" snarled Solb.

"What do we care about Zato?" growled Fasso.

"How long must this last? How long?" howled Solb.

Fasso reared and hurled himself against the bars, growling. "It must end any moment, any moment. . . ."

Solb rolled on the floor. "We will be free!" he muttered, "Free! Free!"

"We must be free! Must be free!" howled Fasso.

"We are waiting! Waiting! Waiting!" cried Solb.

They had been captured separately about a year before. They were brought together on the ship and had been in the zoo only three months. They refused to believe that their present state was in any way unalterable or final.

"We are waiting! We are waiting!" They kept growling, snarling, whining confidently or furiously, hopefully or desperately.

Vasta stole away. No success in that quarter.

The panthers continued their dance.

Then Vasta heard loud and piteous howls. She had stopped under a board and was wondering where she should go next, to whom she should impart her news, when she heard these cries. Vasta knew that voice and also that cry of pain. It was her friend, the gentle, friendly wolf, the only creature among all those in the zoo whom she had ever been able to approach without fear. He cried so that her blood froze, howled so horribly that her heart stood still. Vasta was terrified at the thought of what might be happening in that cage, the mere idea made her shudder. But she was unable to withstand the alarming appeal of that voice. Sympathy, excitement, curiosity urged her on. She ran without stopping to think, as if in the grip of a dream, disregarding all caution. She flitted over open gravel paths where people were walking, ran along the ledge

and climbing up, gazed down into the cage with beating heart.

The gentle wolf, Hallo, was lying on the ground
while Talla, the wild female, was taking out her fury
on him. With wildly waving feet, Hallo was striving to
ward her off, trying to escape her cruel fangs. A thin
trickle of blood was running from his body over the
concrete.

Talla was trying to catch Hallo by the throat, and
Hallo was desperately twisting away in pain and fear.

"What did I ever do to you?" he howled.

"You must die!" growled Talla.

"Let me go!" cried Hallo.

"When you are dead, you slave, you traitor!" snarled
Talla.

"Help! He-e-elp!" howled Hallo.

"Coward!" she yelped while her teeth flashed as they
snapped together. But she had bitten nothing but air.

Horrified, bewildered, and terribly excited, Vasta
stared down at the whirling knot of wolves, deafened
by their howls and growls.

Suddenly a big jet of water swished into the cage, caught Talla and hurled her away from her victim. It took away her breath.

"Again!" called the curator to a keeper. "Don't take the hose off her for a minute!"

Once more the jet of water caught Talla's flank, and playing over her body, reached her head, struck her face. Pinned by the column of gushing water, Talla was nearly suffocated. Beside herself with terror, paralyzed by the force of the water, shuddering with cold, she turned tail. She ran the length of the cage, pursued everywhere by the hose.

Hallo meanwhile skulked lamely into the sleeping compartment.

They had set a box over the open door of the cage, and when Talla, totally exhausted at last, rushed in, the curator cried, "Enough!" In a twinkling the jet of water vanished. Talla crouched in the box, feeling with relief that she was saved. She had forgotten her rage.

They closed the box and carried Talla away.

"The poor little fellow," said the curator, "he's no

match for her! We'll put her with the strong Russian wolf. He'll take good care of her."

Hallo licked his wounds, feeling that he too was saved.

"She was unlivable," he told Vasta. "I'm delighted that she's gone! She would have murdered me! She certainly would! And why? I haven't the slightest idea. I was friendly to her."

"Yes," Vasta threw in, "you're always friendly."

"Am I not?" whimpered Hallo. "But she—she's mean! She wouldn't let me out in the cage at all. I had to stay in here and never go near her. That was impossible. With the best will in the world, it was impossible. See what she did to me. . . ."

It was a long time before Vasta took leave of Hallo. Now she had a second piece of news. But it was not to be the last.

When she got to the fox (she didn't know exactly why she should rush right off to her enemy), the cage was empty.

She sniffed cautiously around the bars. A strange

scent reached her nostrils. Vasta chanced it and ran by fits and starts right across the perilous open space, watchful and ready to flee at any moment. But the strange scent drew her on.

There was not a sound from the artificial lair. Only silence, utter silence.

Vasta trembled and ran a little bit further, and peered in.

The fox was lying stiff and cold. His face was pressed close against the wall. It looked peaceful.

Vasta the mouse hurried away.

Now she had three interesting bits of news.

Chapter Twenty

"Which Do You Like Better?"

EVENING WAS FALLING. ELIZA WAS putting Peter the chimpanzee to sleep and Karl was standing beside her, glowering down.

"Yes, my friend," Eliza continued, "you don't fool me one little bit. It's a disgrace the way you treat those poor bears!"

Karl laughed scornfully. "A disgrace! Very well, let it be a disgrace!"

"It certainly is," Eliza insisted. She gave her hand

to Peter who played gently with her fingers as he fell asleep. "That's what it is, a disgrace! I know what I'm talking about!"

"Well, then, why don't you call it a crime and be done with it!" said Karl bitterly. He knew he was in the wrong and it made him the more obstinate.

"Well, since you say so yourself," Eliza retorted, "it is a crime!"

"Eliza!"

"Ssh!" she admonished. "Quiet, Peter is trying to sleep."

"Oh, what do I care about Peter?"

"You and your 'what do I cares'!" she interrupted angrily. "That's what you say about the bears, too!"

"The bears! Dirty, tricky, mean beasts, those bears!"

"Indeed!" Eliza was becoming more exasperated. "And you don't think at all about the fact that they're prisoners. It never occurs to you that they're mean because you hurt them!"

"Of course," he growled, "of course! It's all my fault! And those scoundrels, those dirty rascals, they're not

THE CITY JUNGLE ❧ 271

to blame at all! They're just little baa-lambs, I suppose!"

"Nobody supposes that bears are baa-lambs," said Eliza in a voice that suddenly grew very soft. "But stop to think, Karl! Nobody is doing you any injustice. . . ."

"Oh no?" Karl laughed bitterly. "I suppose the way you're treating me is no injustice, then?"

"I can't be nice to you," said Eliza earnestly, "I can't when you . . ." Her eyes were brimming with tears.

"When I beat those beasts!" Karl finished up for her. He was beside himself. He seized her arm and shook her. "Which do you like better, those beasts or me?"

"Let me go," begged Eliza.

"Which do you like better?" Karl shouted.

"Let me go," repeated Eliza. "And take care that the curator doesn't find out how you . . ."

"The curator," Karl sneered, "the curator can go chase himself! I'm asking you now and I want an answer! Do you hear? An answer!"

At that moment Peter sat up. He was disturbed and could not sleep. He started to put his arm around Eliza's shoulder, to protect her and also to protect himself.

But Karl seized him and threw him back furiously on the bed. "Leave us alone!" he shouted. "Leave us alone, you damned ape!"

Peter somersaulted and lay dumbfounded, rolling his big melancholy clever eyes.

Eliza stood between them. "Go!" she commanded. As Karl hesitated she cried again, "Go! That's my answer!"

There was such decision in her voice that Karl turned on his heel and went out, slamming the door.

Chapter Twenty-One

Night Chorus

PITCH BLACK NIGHT SPREAD OVER the zoological garden. The tumult of the sleepless city reached it only as a distant confused rumbling. Its electric lights throbbed as a pale glow against the sky a-glitter with a thousand stars.

In the zoo arose the sound of voices.

Voices from Africa and Asia, from the polar ice and the jungles of India, from the grassy plains of Tanganyika and the primeval forests of Borneo.

They were all gathered here, and all cried, whimpered and raged with longing for their homes.

Lions groaned and tigers moaned as if their breasts would burst.

Elephants trumpeted like thunder.

Polar bears roared and the brown bears roared furiously with them.

Wolves howled in long-drawn plaints.

Hyenas burst out in shrill laughter.

Monkeys screeched.

All cried the same thing. How long must we remain captive? What have we done that we should suffer so horribly? Why are we here? Why?

Sudden silence.

In the darkness of the zoo lights are moving, lights like stars that have fallen from some fabulous heaven and are wandering about here on earth.

But these were no stars. There was no fabulous heaven in the zoo. Perhaps there is none anywhere—or only in the hearts of the children of men when very small and innocent.

The flashing lights gleamed always in pairs. Two by two, close together.

Anyone who knew the zoo would have recognized that these were the eyes of the captives, gleaming from the darkness of their cages as if ablaze with expectation and impatient longing.

There were big eyes that flashed like precious magic amber; others that shimmered a weird emerald green; others whose gleam was shot with sparks of red, blue and gold. And there were little eyes that were like rockets just before they flare out, and others that glowed as red as boiling hot blood.

All seemed to hover suspended, free and motionless, in the night air. Two by two they hung suspended, close to the ground, or at varying levels above the earth. But all signified one thing—life, expectation, longing.

For several moments the captives were silent as if awaiting the response to their frantic outcries, their wild plaints, their impatient demands.

The burning eyes stared into the darkness of the night and into the darkness of fate.

Then a single howl arose, and others joined it, groaning. Others whined or roared their fervent pleas. Once more all were united, friend and foe, weak and strong, all were alike in impotence, in desperation.

Their chorus of lamentation did not reach the ears of people enjoying themselves or sleeping the sleep of the just.

The chorus of the captives mounted to the stars.

But the stars twinkled and gleamed and glittered and remained mute.